She's naked!

"'The Spirit of Sweet Valley' could never have been painted without a woman who gave her all for this vision," Dakota said, looking straight at Jessica. "Jessica Wakefield." He gestured toward her, and she smiled.

"Thank you, Dakota. You've captured a side of me that few people have ever seen," Jessica said, glancing around the room.

Dakota pulled the gold-colored cord that was attached to the red drape, dramatically revealing the painting that everyone had gathered to view. Immediately the room was filled with the sound of a collective gasp.

Jessica's jaw dropped, and tears sprang to her eyes. Next to her, Lila's eyes widened, and she giggled. Patty had a shocked expression on her face.

"She's naked!" Elizabeth exclaimed.

Francine Pascal's

SWEET VALLEY
High™

CALIFORNIA LOVE

by the editors of Sweet Valley High

BANTAM BOOKS
NEW YORK · TORONTO · LONDON · SYDNEY · AUCKLAND

RL 6, age 12 and up

CALIFORNIA LOVE

A Bantam Book / October 1995

Based on the teleplays © 1994, 1995 InterProd, Inc.

Sweet Valley High®
is a registered trademark of Francine Pascal
Conceived by Francine Pascal
Produced by Daniel Weiss Associates, Inc.
33 West 17th Street
New York, NY 10011

ISBN: 0-553-57011-0

Published simultaneously in the United States and Canada

Bantam Books are published by Bantam Books, a division of Bantam
Doubleday Dell Publishing Group, Inc. Its trademark, consisting of the
words "Bantam Books" and the portrayal of a rooster, is Registered in
U.S. Patent and Trademark Office and in other countries. Marca
Registrada. Bantam Books, 1540 Broadway, New York, New York 10036.

PRINTED IN THE UNITED STATES OF AMERICA

OPM   0 9 8 7 6 5 4 3 2 1

CALIFORNIA LOVE

Contents

Introduction

Dear Readers,

You may have read about Jessica and Elizabeth Wakefield in the Sweet Valley High paperback series, and you've probably tuned in to the popular Sweet Valley High Series on TV. Well, we've decided to bring you the best of both worlds. We got our hands on some Sweet Valley High TV series scripts and turned them into stories, or novelizations. So now you can not only watch your favorite twins on TV, you can read all about your favorite episodes!

For those of you diehard fans out there, you might recognize that some of the plots of the TV series were taken from Sweet Valley High books. Can you guess which ones?

We hope you enjoy these stories as much as we did.

—The editors of Sweet Valley High

DANGEROUS LOVE

Based on the teleplay by Josh Goldstein
Story by Josh Goldstein and Jonathon Prince

Jessica Wakefield noticed that the Sweet Valley High parking lot was almost full by the time her twin sister, Elizabeth, pulled the red Jeep into a free spot. Even sitting in the Jeep, Jessica could hear music from the homecoming dance blasting from the gymnasium.

Jessica grinned. In just a few short hours she would be crowned homecoming queen, and all the eyes of Sweet Valley High would be turned to her. *As usual*, she thought happily.

Elizabeth switched off the ignition and unbuckled her seat belt. "Good luck tonight, Jessica," Elizabeth said, smiling at her twin.

"I don't think I'll need it," Jessica responded smugly.

Although Elizabeth was one of the nominees for the homecoming queen title, Jessica didn't see her as serious competition. The twins might have

1

been identical, but when it came to style, Jessica knew she had her sister beat by a mile. Wearing a short black skirt and matching cropped shirt, Jessica was sure she looked sizzling-hot. And her hair was curled and swept alluringly on top of her head—the perfect style for a queen!

The twins walked into the crowded gym together, but they separated immediately, each searching out her friends.

Jessica found Patty Gilbert and Lila Fowler, two of her best friends. The girls stood off to the side of the dance floor, where they could view the crowd.

"Elizabeth! I voted for you," said a shy-looking student, approaching Jessica.

Jessica cast the girl a scathing glance. "That's nice to know," she responded sarcastically. "But I'm Jessica. Elizabeth's over there somewhere." She waved in her sister's general direction.

"Oh. Sorry. You look so much alike," the girl said.

"Wow! I never noticed." Jessica rolled her eyes. Since when did identical twins *not* look alike?

"Your sister seems to have cornered the nerd vote," Lila commented dryly as the girl skipped off toward Elizabeth.

Jessica shrugged. She knew she had the contest in the bag. There was no reason to begrudge Elizabeth a few useless votes.

"Hey, Jessica, we still on for tomorrow night?" A tall, good-looking guy had appeared at Jessica's side.

"As long as you voted for me, and I win," Jessica said.

"Oh, you will. I voted for you three times," he answered, giving her a thumbs-up sign as he dissolved into the crowd.

"Three times?" Patty repeated, raising her eyebrows.

"Nothing like school spirit," Jessica said.

"How many dates for votes did you promise?" Lila asked. She was swaying in time to the loud music, and her black dress moved gracefully around her legs.

"Lila, I am really insulted." Jessica tried to look hurt. So what if she *had* made some false promises to secure votes? All was fair in love and war. And the homecoming queen contest definitely qualified as war!

Elizabeth stood near the refreshment table, absent-mindedly sipping a cup of punch. She was wearing a pretty flowered minidress and her favorite pink cropped cardigan, but she was frowning. Elizabeth really wasn't in the mood for a dance, especially one without Todd Wilkins. But she and her longtime boyfriend had just broken up, so Elizabeth was doomed to spend homecoming alone. Her spirits picked up a little bit when she saw Enid Rollins heading toward her across the dance floor.

"How are you holding up?" Enid asked, her voice filled with concern.

Elizabeth smiled at Enid, noticing how lovely her best friend looked with her auburn hair curled delicately around her face.

"Okay. It's just kind of hard to be here without Todd," Elizabeth answered. She was unable to keep the sadness out of her voice.

"Don't look now," Enid whispered. "But he's over there."

Elizabeth started to follow Enid's gaze, but her friend stopped her.

"Not now," Enid said.

Elizabeth waited impatiently for Enid to give her the go-ahead. Even though she didn't want Todd to catch her looking, she was dying to see him.

"Okay, now," Enid said finally.

Elizabeth turned her head at the exact moment that Todd turned in their direction. "No," Enid cried, quickly reversing her instructions.

But it was too late. Once Elizabeth's eyes met Todd's, she couldn't make herself look away. They stared at each other for a moment, and Elizabeth felt her heart constrict painfully. She couldn't deny that she still loved Todd. She turned away sadly.

When Enid asked Elizabeth for the details

about why she'd ended things with Todd, Elizabeth bit her lip, trying to think of a way to explain. There was so much to say.

"He wants to make all my decisions for me," Elizabeth began. "He's been doing it for weeks. I felt . . . smothered."

"I wouldn't mind being smothered by a guy like Todd," Enid said, her voice dreamy.

"You don't get it, Enid. On top of everything else, he put me up for homecoming queen without asking me." Elizabeth frowned as she remembered how angry she'd been when Todd told her the news.

"Why didn't you pull out?" Enid asked.

"I tried, but the ballots were already printed by the time I found out."

"What's the big deal?" Enid took a big swallow of punch and regarded Elizabeth steadily.

"These things are just popularity contests. They're so shallow." Elizabeth sighed. On top of breaking up with Todd, she couldn't believe she was involved in something as outdated and antifeminist as a homecoming queen contest.

Todd and Winston Egbert, dressed in jackets and ties, stood across the room from Elizabeth and Enid. Todd watched Elizabeth's beautiful face, wishing more than anything that he could walk over and put his arms around her. He loved Elizabeth, and they belonged together.

"I can't believe Liz broke up with me over such a little thing," Todd complained to Winston. "All I did was nominate her for homecoming queen."

Todd had thought he was doing Elizabeth a *favor* when he put her on the ballot. He'd just wanted her to know that he thought she was the most awesome girl in school.

"Too bad women don't come with instructions," Winston said, putting a comforting hand on Todd's shoulder.

Todd nodded sadly. Right about now, he would have given anything for an instruction manual.

"I am so psyched to be homecoming queen," Jessica said to Patty and Lila. She surveyed the gym, imagining herself promenading around with the homecoming crown on her head.

"You're not queen yet," Lila pointed out.

"What are you talking about?" Jessica asked. "See those twenty guys over there with their tongues hanging out? They're my loyal subjects."

Jessica moved in time to the music, aware that any guy watching her would give his left leg for a chance to dance with her. Suddenly her gaze fell on a guy who had just walked into the room. He was the definition of tall, dark, and handsome— and he looked older than most of the kids at the dance.

"Hey, who's the babe?" Jessica said aloud. She was already plotting how she was going to meet him.

"His name is Scott Daniels," Patty said, lowering her voice to confide the information to Lila and Jessica. "And check this out—he's a freshman in college."

Jessica grinned. "A college guy? Perfect."

"Jess, I don't think he can vote," Lila commented sarcastically.

"It's not his vote I'm interested in," Jessica answered.

The girls' conversation was cut short when a geeky-looking underclassman approached Jessica with a wide smile.

"Hey, Elizabeth, I voted for you," he said cheerfully.

"Get lost, doofus," Jessica responded immediately. She was really getting disgusted with all of these nothings who found it necessary to inform her that they'd voted for her twin.

"Oh . . . sorry, Jessica," the guy said, backing away quickly.

At that moment Bruce Patman's arrogant voice came booming over a microphone that had been set up onstage. Jessica noticed that Bruce looked even better than usual in his white jacket and pale colored shirt.

"Everybody! Please!" Bruce called. The music was shut off and everyone in the huge gym became quiet. "As president of the Sweet Valley High Homecoming Committee, it's my honor to introduce some pretty fine-lookin' women. And now for the crowning of our queen."

Bruce smiled, looking out at the crowd. "Will it be Princess Amy Sutton?" he said dramatically, naming the first of the candidates. Tall and willowy Amy stepped forward and waved at the crowd as everyone clapped.

"Princess Elizabeth Wakefield?" Bruce continued, while Enid clasped Elizabeth's hand and held it high in the air. "Or Princess Jessica Wakefield?" Bruce finished.

Jessica walked forward, swinging her hips. She smiled seductively and waved at the group of guys who were hooting and cheering for her. In just seconds, Jessica would be onstage and graciously accepting the title of homecoming queen. She couldn't wait.

"Manuel, some royal tunes, please," Bruce said, gesturing toward Manny Lopez, who was acting as the dance's deejay.

"You got it," Manny answered, popping a compact disk into his CD player in preparation for the queen's dance with her king.

"And this year's homecoming queen is . . ." Bruce paused.

"I love being me," Jessica said to Patty and Lila. She started walking toward the stage, blowing kisses at the people in her path.

"Elizabeth Wakefield!" Bruce shouted into the microphone.

Jessica stopped in her tracks, glowering. She'd never felt so humiliated. Her moment in the limelight had been stolen from her by her very own twin sister!

Her heart in her feet, Jessica watched as Enid gave Elizabeth a quick hug. Then Elizabeth walked onto the stage, where Bruce placed the traditional rhinestone tiara on her head. Finally Elizabeth moved to the podium where Bruce had been standing. She bent over so that she could speak directly into the microphone.

"Thank you very much," Elizabeth said. The room exploded with cheers and applause. "This is quite a surprise. I never really thought of myself as a homecoming queen." She sounded so sweet and innocent that Jessica felt like throwing up.

"Of course, no queen would be complete without her king," Bruce said, stepping back up to the microphone. "And this year's honor goes to . . . Winston Egbert?" The amazement and distaste in Bruce's voice was obvious. Winston wasn't exactly Sweet Valley High's number-one stud.

Jessica rolled her eyes as she watched Winston jump onto the stage amid cheering and laughter. But at least Winston winning king made her feel a little better about Elizabeth having beaten her out. Jessica would rather die than dance with Winston.

On the stage, Winston ducked his head so that Elizabeth could place the large red and gold crown on his head. When Elizabeth kissed his cheek, Winston's eyes lit up. Then he bounded over to the microphone.

"Go, Winston!" Enid shouted from the dance floor.

"Thank you! Next to the time in third grade when I kissed Lila Fowler, this is the happiest day of my life!"

"It never happened, I swear," Lila yelled out.

"As my first official decree as king," Winston continued, "I declare all laboratory rats liberated." He paused, then turned to Bruce. "Bruce, you're free to go."

Bruce scowled at Winston, who raised his arms over his head and shouted, "Long live the king!"

Obviously struggling to maintain his calm, Bruce shoved Winston away from the microphone and took his place. "Okay, it's time for the royal couple to take the floor. Manny, kick it!"

"Okay, let's open it up," Manny called. He fired up the music, and the gym was immediately pulsating with a fast dance tune.

Elizabeth and Winston began dancing with enthusiasm, moving well together. Once they got warmed up, their moves got more and more outrageous. The crowd clapped and whistled. On the sidelines, Todd stood frowning. He could barely stand to watch Elizabeth dancing with another guy—even if that guy *was* Winston Egbert.

When Winston picked up Elizabeth and swung her around, the rest of the students decided to join in. Soon the dance floor was packed with couples. Jessica watched the whole scene, and for once in her life she didn't feel like dancing.

The music changed from a fast song to a slow and romantic one. Out of nowhere, Winston appeared before Jessica. His crown was balanced precariously on his head, and he looked—in Jessica's opinion—totally ridiculous. He placed a hand on her elbow and tried to steer her toward the dance floor.

"In your dreams, Winston," she said bitingly.

"Who told you about those?" he asked, his voice high and nervous.

Jessica rolled her eyes yet again. This night was not turning out the way she'd planned.

"Dance?" Elizabeth asked Todd softly. She'd found him standing in a corner, looking forlorn.

"Are you still mad?" he asked.

Elizabeth sighed. "My having won doesn't change the fact that we still have a problem."

"I thought you were having fun up there," Todd said defensively.

"That's not the point," Elizabeth insisted. All of a sudden she remembered exactly why she'd

11

been so irritated with Todd's behavior recently. He hadn't tried to understand what she was really feeling. "You just don't get it, do you?"

"I guess not," Todd answered bitterly. "Let's just forget it. I don't feel like dancing." He stomped off, leaving Elizabeth alone and feeling deflated.

"He's making a big mistake," said a voice at her side. She turned and saw a gorgeous older guy standing right next to her. "Dance?" he asked.

Elizabeth's eyes followed Todd's retreating back. Dancing with another guy would serve him right.

"Sure," she answered, although she still felt hesitant. She moved into the stranger's arms, following his lead onto the dance floor. He moved gracefully, and Elizabeth actually began to enjoy herself.

"I'm Scott," he said, pulling her closer.

Elizabeth craned her neck so that she could get a glimpse of where Todd had gone. He caught her eye, then banged out the gymnasium door. Trying not to care that Todd had just left—possibly for good—Elizabeth gave Scott her full attention.

On the other side of the room, Jessica was fuming. "She gets the homecoming queen title *and* a hunk," she pouted. "I'll never live this down."

Days later, Elizabeth sat at the desk in her room trying to write her weekly column for the

Oracle. Usually the words flowed easily when she wrote for the newspaper. But that day was different. All she could think about was how lonely she was without her boyfriend. "I really miss Todd," she typed on the keyboard. Then she sighed heavily.

Without warning, the door that led to the bathroom she shared with Jessica swung open. Jessica sauntered up to Elizabeth's desk and threw a magazine down next to the computer. Elizabeth glanced up, slightly annoyed that Jessica had interrupted her self-pity party.

"What do you think?" Jessica asked.

Elizabeth looked down at the magazine, which was one of the worst on the market. Normally she'd never even allow such a piece of journalistic trash into her room. "Well, it's hack writing," she began, ready to list the many things wrong with the publication.

"I'm talking about the ad," Jessica said impatiently. She walked over to Elizabeth's full-length mirror. "The new WonderBra. It can give *anyone* cleavage." She studied herself in the mirror. She was wearing tight black shorts and a form-fitting red T-shirt.

Her sister sighed. In Elizabeth's opinion, inventions such as the WonderBra set the women's movement back several decades. "Jessica, quit obsessing about your body. It's the same as mine," she said reasonably.

"Yeah . . . but if I just had this bra, it would transform my life." Jessica pivoted in the mirror, admiring herself.

"Get a grip," Elizabeth said, shaking her head. Sometimes her twin really went off the deep end—or, more accurately, off the *shallow* end.

Before Jessica could respond, the phone on Elizabeth's desk rang. "Hello?" After a brief pause to listen, Elizabeth nodded. "Yes, this is Elizabeth. Scott? Sure, I remember."

"Scott from homecoming?" Jessica asked excitedly. She had approached the desk and now was hovering over Elizabeth.

"Friday night? I-I don't know," Elizabeth stammered into the phone. Jessica was practically breathing down her neck, and she was having a hard time concentrating.

Even though she and Todd had officially broken up, she hadn't even considered dating someone else. She was still in love with Todd.

"No, it's just that I . . . I've sort of been seeing someone," Elizabeth explained to Scott. "Yeah, Todd Wilkins. We kind of broke up, but—"

"Are you crazy?" Jessica interrupted.

Elizabeth looked at her sister. "What is your problem?" she snapped. When she realized Scott had thought she was talking to him, she hastened to clear up the misunderstanding. "No, not you, Scott. Could you hold on for a sec?" She covered the receiver with her hand and glared at Jessica. "*What?*"

14

"You're not turning Scott down?" Jessica asked, her voice filled with disbelief.

"But what about Todd?" Elizabeth asked.

"Todd's toast," Jessica said dismissively. "Last I remember, he blew you off at the dance."

Elizabeth nodded to herself. Jessica was right. There was no reason she should give up a date for Todd's sake. "Scott? Yeah . . . Friday would be great."

Elizabeth breathed deeply. She was taking a big step, and she felt nervous. It had been a long time since she'd gone out with another guy.

"Sure, give me your number," she said to Scott, grabbing a pen off the desk.

One thing was for sure—Friday night would be very, very interesting.

Thursday afternoon Elizabeth and Enid walked down the hall of Sweet Valley High. Elizabeth and Todd had been avoiding each other for days, but Elizabeth was determined not to let her sadness show.

"Look at the Eyes and Ears column today," Enid said, holding out the *Oracle* for Elizabeth to see. "'Which star dunker and roving Sweet Valley reporter are no longer playing one-on-one?' Who writes this gossip, anyway?"

Enid was reading from the anonymous Eyes and Ears column that appeared in every issue of the school newspaper. Trying to discover who

15

wrote the gossip column was a favorite pastime of Sweet Valley High students. Elizabeth smiled enigmatically.

"Who knows?" she said.

"Come on, you work for the school paper," Enid coaxed. "You must know."

"Nope." Elizabeth shook her head. "And I wouldn't want to be whoever it is. You know the tradition—if you're found out, you get dumped into the pool."

"Well, there's never anything about me in here," Enid complained. "If I don't get a boyfriend by my birthday, I swear I'll put a personal ad in the *Oracle*." Enid paused, then rattled off her ad. "Shy, sensitive girl looking for Mr. Right. Have car. Will relocate."

Elizabeth laughed, and Enid looked at her, a mischievous twinkle in her eye. "What would you write?" Enid asked.

"Hot babe seeks meaningful relationship with—"

"Anyone!" Enid finished for her. "Thanks, Liz. I'm placing that ad right now."

Enid disappeared into the *Oracle* office just as Elizabeth noticed Todd walking down the hall toward her. He was wearing his red basketball practice uniform, and he looked better than ever. Elizabeth's heart gave a little flutter when he got close.

"Todd," she said, trying to sound casual.

"Elizabeth. Hi." Todd's voice was soft, and he

was gazing into her eyes. "How's it going?"

"Okay, I guess," she answered, dropping her gaze and studying the sleeve of her sweater.

"Great." Todd was silent for a moment, and he seemed to be searching for the right words. "Uh, look, I've been thinking. I owe you an apology."

"Thanks," Elizabeth said. She reached forward and gave him a warm hug. Being back in his arms was the most wonderful feeling in the world. "I'm glad you finally understand how I feel."

"Yeah. I should have danced with you."

Elizabeth looked at him, baffled. He really had no idea what went on in her mind. "Todd, this isn't about *dancing*."

"Whatever it is, can't we just forget about it? Let's go to a movie tomorrow night." He stroked her hands and looked at her pleadingly.

"I can't. I have plans." Elizabeth's voice was tight, and she was having a difficult time holding back her tears.

"Plans? Plans with who?" Todd asked suspiciously. His blue eyes were dark and intense.

"Scott Daniels," she answered.

"Fine. Suit yourself." Todd turned away without another word.

As Elizabeth watched him leave she wondered if she'd just made the biggest mistake of her life.

Thursday after school Jessica was on her bed, holding a portable phone to her ear and smiling.

"Hi, is Scott there?" she said.

A moment later she heard a low, husky voice say hello. "Hi, Scott? It's me, Elizabeth." Jessica was using her best Elizabeth voice, and she knew there was no way Scott would question her identity.

"Look, I thought it might be easier if I met you over at your place. . . . Phi Gamma Alpha? Yeah, I know where that is." Jessica nodded. "See you tomorrow, Scott."

She hung up the phone, then lounged against her pillows. At the thought of her date, her heart pounded with anticipation.

"How do I look?" Elizabeth asked, walking into Jessica's room. It was Friday night, and Elizabeth had spent almost half an hour getting ready for her date with Scott Daniels. She was wearing a summery green dress and her pink cardigan. She'd even put on a little makeup.

"You're wearing that?" Jessica asked disdainfully.

Elizabeth glanced down at herself. "You don't like it?"

"It screams librarian," Jessica said, walking toward her. "Come on, Scott's a college guy. Lose the sweater."

"But I like this sweater," Elizabeth protested, pulling it closer around her. She should have known better than to ask Jessica's advice on fashion.

"Obviously—you wear it every day. It's so . . . *you*." Jessica wrinkled her nose. Then she opened her closet and pulled out a short red leather jacket. "Here."

"This?" Elizabeth asked doubtfully as she put it on. She felt like a walking fire truck.

"You look great. You look like me," Jessica said with satisfaction. "Now all you need is a bit of makeup."

"I already put it on."

"As they say, practice makes perfect." Jessica pushed Elizabeth back into the bathroom.

When Elizabeth was gone, Jessica held the pink sweater up to herself in the mirror. "Yuck!" she exclaimed.

An hour later Elizabeth sat on the stairs of the Wakefield home, waiting for Scott to pick her up. By now she'd read the same magazine three times. She'd never had a guy be so late for a date, and she didn't like the feeling one bit.

Elizabeth glanced at her watch one last time, then threw down the magazine. It seemed as if Scott Daniels was going to be a no-show.

"Forget it," she said aloud, throwing off Jessica's red leather jacket.

Elizabeth grabbed the keys to the Jeep and headed for the front door. She needed some air— and she needed it now.

*   *   *

19

Jessica's taxi pulled up in front of the sprawling Phi Gamma Alpha house. The porch that ran along the front of the fraternity house was overflowing with college kids. A big banner reading PARTY TONIGHT hung from the second-floor balcony. Although the house was a little old and the paint was peeling, Jessica couldn't wait to get inside.

She'd pulled Elizabeth's sweater on over her own tight black dress, and she'd been practicing her twin's voice. But as soon as the time was right she'd let Scott know exactly how lucky he was. After all, no guy in his right mind would prefer Elizabeth to Jessica.

Jessica surveyed the big living room as she walked into the crowded fraternity. Lots of people were dancing, and several couples were kissing on the beat-up sofas.

She found Scott almost immediately, and he smiled brightly. "Elizabeth! Wow, you look amazing."

"Thanks. Sorry I'm late. I wound up having to get a ride." Jessica noticed that Scott looked just as handsome as he had the night of the homecoming dance. In jeans and a blue sweater, he was the ultimate college guy.

"I'll get you home later," he responded easily. "How about a drink? We've got everything. Wine, beer—"

"Diet cola?" she interrupted. Jessica never

20

drank alcohol, and she wasn't about to start now.

"A diet cola?" Scott asked, looking a little bewildered. "I'll have to check."

An hour later, Jessica was having the time of her life. So far, her date with Scott was going great. Now they were dancing to some loud, pulsating music, and Jessica saw that several guys were casting admiring glances her way.

"I really love the way you move, Liz," Scott said in a low voice.

Jessica executed a perfect spin. She'd peeled off her sister's sweater, and now she looked totally amazing in her tight dress. "Thanks. Jessica taught me everything I know. She's an awesome dancer." She figured she'd start pumping the *real* love of Scott's life while the night was still young.

"Let's take a break for a second," Scott said. "I need another drink."

Jessica nodded, and they started moving off the dance floor. They stopped when another frat brother bumped into Scott. The guy gave Jessica an appreciative once-over.

"Whoa," the guy said. Then he whistled softly.

"Hey, Rick, this is the girl I was telling you about," Scott said.

"I'm . . . Elizabeth," Jessica said to him, giving him her hand.

"Killer," Rick said.

Jessica felt the heat of Rick's stare on her back as she and Scott headed toward the door.

Elizabeth had parked the Jeep near a small lake that was one of her favorite spots in Sweet Valley. This had always been a special place for her and Todd, and she liked to come here when she needed to reflect about life. As Elizabeth got closer to the lake she saw a lone figure throwing pebbles into the calm water. Just as she'd secretly been hoping, Todd had come to the lake as well. He turned away from the shoreline, and she saw that he was staring at an old tree on which both of their initials were carved inside a large heart.

"I remember when you carved that," she said, coming up behind him. "It was after the Fourth of July barbecue at Fowler Crest."

Todd's eyes flew to her. "What are you doing here?" he asked coldly.

"Sometimes I come up here to think. Good memories." She walked toward him, so that he had to look her straight in the eye.

"Yeah. So what happened to your date with what's-his-face?"

"I canceled it," Elizabeth lied quickly. Then she decided she had to tell him the truth. "Well . . . actually, he stood me up."

Todd didn't react. It was almost as if he hadn't heard her. "What did I do that was so wrong?"

"You took me for granted," Elizabeth explained. She really wanted Todd to understand what she was trying to communicate.

"That's crazy," he said.

"No, it's not." Elizabeth desperately wanted to find a way to make him listen to her—*really* listen. "Lately you're always making decisions for me. What movies we see. Which parties we go to."

"I thought we were a team," Todd said, his voice serious.

"This isn't a game, Todd. It's *us*. For our relationship to work, we have to talk. We have to be equal partners."

"I didn't realize I was doing that. I guess I screwed up," Todd said. He moved closer to her, and his eyes were sad. "Liz, you're the best thing that's ever happened to me. I don't want to fight with you. I love you."

Elizabeth felt her eyes dampen. "I love you too, Todd."

Without needing to say another word, they put their arms around each other. Todd kissed Elizabeth, hugging her as close as he could. Under a shining moon and a sky full of stars, Elizabeth sighed happily. And she mentally thanked Scott Daniels for having stood her up. This had turned out to be one of the best nights of her life.

"This is so cool," Jessica said. She and Scott were dancing slowly, and she had her arms wrapped around his neck.

"Yeah, we have one of these parties every month," Scott said. She could feel his warm hands on her back.

"You should invite my twin sister, Jessica, next time. This is totally her scene," she said, trying to lay the groundwork for informing Scott of her real identity.

"Great, double my pleasure." Scott grinned at Jessica, but he didn't seem to be paying much attention to what she was saying.

"No, I mean you'll probably like Jessica better than me. All the guys at school want to date her," Jessica said truthfully.

"If she looks just like you, I can see why." Scott pulled her closer, and Jessica gazed into his eyes.

"Yeah, but I'm so, you know, conservative," Jessica said slowly. "Jessica's more your type. I'll be happy to set you up with her anytime."

Scott raised his eyebrows. "I'll keep it in mind. How about another drink?"

"Sure," Jessica agreed. "Then I've got something to tell you."

In the Moon Beach Café, some of the Sweet Valley High gang was listening to one of Bruce's characteristically self-centered stories.

"It was one of the most difficult decisions of my life," Bruce said. He shook some salt onto his french fries and smiled smugly. "Sure, my

24

Porsche is fast, it's high-performance, it's got great lines, and, face it, it's a babe magnet—"

"Is there a point to this story?" Patty interrupted.

Bruce was standing next to Enid and Patty's booth. Now he put one foot on the seat and leaned forward. "I bought myself a four-wheel-drive, totally loaded . . . switch on the fly, full roll cage, KC Daylighters."

"What do you need a second car for?" Enid asked.

"One for him and one for his ego," Winston said. He'd been sitting on a stool at the counter, but up until now he'd been silent.

Patty and Enid laughed, but Bruce was *not* amused. "You're a riot, Eggbeater." Bruce strolled over to the counter. "Here's a quarter," he said, flipping a coin at Winston. "Buy yourself a personality. *Hasta*, pinheads."

Bruce walked out of the Moon Beach Café as if he were the king of the world.

"I can't wait to see that guy on *Lifestyles of the Rich and Boring*," Winston said, sliding into the booth with the girls.

While Patty and Enid giggled, Lila came rushing up to the table. As always, she was dressed in a chic designer outfit, and she had a jaunty black beret on her head. She also looked as if she were about to burst with news.

"Guys, guys," she said excitedly. "Wait till you

hear this. I just found out who writes the Eyes and Ears gossip column."

"Who?" Patty asked, her eyes widening.

"My sources are totally reliable," Lila told them with a conspiratorial glance. "I saw Ginny down at the mall a little while ago, and she said her sister's boyfriend found out from this guy." She stopped and took a breath, then plunged back into her story. "I think he's on the swim team—anyway, his girlfriend's locker is right next to Mr. Collins's office, and she saw someone we know hand him an envelope after hours, and—"

"Lila!" Enid shouted impatiently.

"Elizabeth Wakefield," Lila announced dramatically. Her red hair swung around her face as she jumped up and down.

"Oh, right. I'm sure she would write all about her and Todd. Please." Enid snorted with disgust. Lila's gossip could get really out of hand sometimes.

"Wake up and smell the cappuccino, guys," Lila insisted. "Mr. Collins, after hours, envelope. It's *totally* suspicious."

"Shh! Here she comes," Winston whispered.

"Liz? Todd? What are you guys doing together?" Enid called to Elizabeth and Todd, who had just walked into the Moon Beach holding hands and smiling.

"Let's just say that things worked out the way

they were supposed to," Elizabeth answered. She smiled as Todd hugged her close.

"What'd you do, kill Scott Daniels?" Winston asked.

"I didn't have to," Todd said, looking extremely relieved about that fact.

"Scott totally flaked," Elizabeth explained to the group. "And I'm *really* glad." She kissed Todd gently on the cheek.

"He wasn't right for you, anyway," Enid commented. "Can I have his number?"

Elizabeth laughed at her best friend's one-track mind.

"So, rumor has it you write the Eyes and Ears column," Patty said, sounding amused.

"We've got it from a reliable source," Lila added defensively.

"Yeah, some guy on the swim team." Enid's tone was dry, and she was looking at Lila as if she were crazy.

"Who may have a brother—or was it a sister?—who lives in a locker down by the *Oracle* office," Patty added.

"You guys are so dense," Lila said, her blue eyes flashing.

An older guy had walked into the Moon Beach with a girl on each arm. The guy came up to Elizabeth and leered at her.

"Do the Phi Gams throw a great bash or what?" he asked, grinning.

"I don't know. I wasn't there," Elizabeth said. Confusion was written all over her face.

"Sure you were. You're . . . uh . . . Elizabeth, right?" the guy responded.

"Yeah." Elizabeth stepped a little closer to Todd.

"I met you tonight with Scott Daniels."

"She's been with me all night," Todd said. The muscles in his jaw had clenched at the mention of Scott's name.

Suddenly Todd and Elizabeth looked at each other.

"Jessica," they said in unison.

Jessica watched Scott pour her another diet cola, admiring the view. They were in a small room of the fraternity house, and nobody else was around.

"I can't believe you're only sixteen," Scott said, sitting down next to Jessica on the couch.

"Why not?" Jessica asked.

"I don't know. You're just so mature." Scott reached over and touched the strap of Jessica's dress. She pulled away, irritated that he was being so forward.

"Drink up," Scott said, rubbing Jessica's shoulder.

Jessica took a sip of the drink, then grimaced. "What did you put in here?" she asked angrily.

"Just a little rum," Scott said casually. "It'll loosen you up."

"I don't need to be loosened up," Jessica said,

indignant. "Let's just dance." She put down her drink and tried to stand up, but Scott grabbed her arm and pulled her back down beside him.

"We've *been* dancing. Why don't we go upstairs to my room and . . . talk?" Scott stroked Jessica's hair and gave her a suggestive grin.

"I don't think so," Jessica said, rising again. When Scott pulled on her arm, she became furious. "Ow! Quit it!" she yelled.

He ignored her, running his fingers through her long blond hair. "So what did you want to tell me?" he asked.

"Forget it. You blew it." Jessica looked at him with disgust, but he leaned over and kissed her on the lips.

She jerked away, then threw her drink over his head. "You're such a pig," she shouted before she stalked away.

"You're so high school, Elizabeth," Scott called after her.

Jessica turned around, fuming. "And by the way, I'm not Elizabeth, I'm Jessica, jerk."

Jessica slammed the door behind her, hoping she'd never have to lay eyes on Scott Daniels again. But she still had one problem. How was she going to get home?

Todd and Elizabeth pulled the Jeep up to the Phi Gamma house. It was obvious that the party was still in full swing.

"You sure you wanna go in there?" Todd asked Elizabeth, eyeing the drunken college kids who were hanging out on the porch.

Elizabeth nodded. "I can't wait to see the look on her face when I do."

Suddenly Jessica burst out of the house and stormed across the yard. "Speak of the devil," Todd said.

"Leaving so soon?" Elizabeth called sarcastically.

Then she noticed that Jessica looked pale, and her eyes were red and puffy. If Elizabeth didn't know better, she'd have thought that her twin had been crying. "What happened?" she asked. "You look terrible."

"Scott tried to get me drunk, and then he grabbed me," Jessica blurted out, her voice cracking.

"Are you okay?" Elizabeth asked, worried. She looked at the house, wondering exactly what had gone on during the party.

"I'm gonna kill that guy!" Todd yelled, preparing to leap out of the car and wring Scott's neck. Jessica might not have been his favorite person, but he wasn't about to let some sleazeball take advantage of her.

"Todd, you're not helping," Elizabeth said forcefully.

"I just want to go home," Jessica sobbed. She climbed into the Jeep, and Elizabeth put the car in gear. She wanted to get as far away from that fraternity house as possible.

A couple of hours later, Elizabeth was lying in her bed, taking notes for her next column in the *Oracle*. She felt as though she wouldn't be able to sleep a wink.

The silence was broken by a knock on her door. "Liz, can I come in?" she heard Jessica say. "Come on, you haven't said anything to me all night."

When Elizabeth didn't answer, Jessica walked in. "Look, I know what I did was wrong. I know I'm the world's worst sister, okay? But I'm really, really sorry."

Jessica sat down next to Elizabeth. In her nightgown she looked vulnerable and sad. "Won't you say something?" she begged. "Come on, give me a break."

"Why should I?" Elizabeth finally asked. She was sick and tired of being manipulated by her twin. Jessica had been totally wrong to steal her date with Scott—even if he had turned out to be a monster.

"Hey, I did it for you," Jessica insisted. "I mean, you really didn't want to go out with Scott, and if I hadn't, you and Todd wouldn't be together right now."

Elizabeth felt herself softening. It was true that Jessica had been indirectly—and inadvertently—responsible for Elizabeth's getting back together with Todd. "You know, I never thought of it that way," she said.

"Yeah. So you forgive me, right?"

"Of course I do," Elizabeth said, hugging her sister. She could never stay mad at her twin for long. Their bond was more important than any silly fight they might get into. But that didn't mean she would let Jessica get away with this stunt *too* easily.

As Jessica cheerfully headed back to her own room, Elizabeth smiled to herself. Soon enough, she'd give Jessica a taste of her own medicine.

Monday at school, Elizabeth stood nervously next to her locker, waiting for Todd. She breathed a sigh of relief as she saw him jogging toward her.

"I took care of everything. It's all set," he said.

Elizabeth nodded. "Oh, here she comes," she whispered. Jessica had just strolled though the door of Sweet Valley High, wearing a pair of jean shorts and a new white tank top.

When Jessica got close to them, Elizabeth saw her glance at another girl who was walking by. "Nice outfit," Jessica said under her breath, looking at the girl as if she were an alien.

"Have a little pity, Jess," Elizabeth scolded her, stepping close to her sister. Then she accidentally-on-purpose spilled the grape juice she was holding all over Jessica's snowy white shirt.

Jessica shrieked. "Omigod! I can't go to class looking like this!"

"I'm sorry, Jess. Here." Elizabeth pulled her pink sweater from her bag and handed it to her twin.

"Not that sweater," Jessica said, rolling her eyes.

"Suit yourself," Elizabeth said casually.

Jessica glanced down at her tank top again. It was completely ruined. "No, no," she sighed. "I'll wear it."

"We're going to be late for class," Todd said.

Elizabeth touched her boyfriend's arm. "I left my homework in the car. I'll see you at lunch." She ran down the hallway as if she were going to race to the parking lot.

Out of nowhere, a huge group of Sweet Valley students came rushing around the corner of the hallway. "There she is!" Lila yelled, pointing at Jessica.

"See you later, *Liz*," Todd said loudly to Jessica, turning to leave.

"What?" Jessica asked, trying to button up the sweater she'd pulled on.

The group descended upon her suddenly, and they quickly picked her up and carried her in the direction of Sweet Valley High's indoor pool. For the second time in five minutes, Jessica shrieked. "What are you doing? Put me down!"

"You know the price for writing the Eyes and Ears column, Liz," Bruce said.

"Hope you can swim," Manny added, and everyone laughed.

"But I'm Jessica, you idiots!" Jessica screamed, trying to kick herself out of their firm grasp.

Lila looked at her. "Nice try. Jessica wouldn't be caught dead in that sweater."

As the group continued to carry her down the hall, Jessica looked over her shoulder. "Elizabeth, I'm gonna kill you!" she shouted.

Elizabeth and Todd had come out from their hiding places and were watching the scene. As they hugged, Elizabeth laughed. Then she heard the sound of a huge splash.

It was true that Elizabeth was the writer of the Eyes and Ears column, and she was thrilled that for once in their lives, *Jessica* was having to pay the price for something *Elizabeth* had done.

As Todd pulled Elizabeth closer and kissed her, she thought how great it was when *everything* worked out exactly as it was supposed to.

ORACLE ON AIR

Based on the teleplay by Raul Fernandez

Sixteen-year-old Jessica Wakefield tossed her long blond hair over her shoulder as she walked down the hallway of Sweet Valley High with her twin sister, Elizabeth.

"I just can't believe what a jerk Dave turned out to be!" Jessica said, scowling at the thought of her latest disaster in the love department.

Elizabeth nodded, turning to look at her sister. "Major jerk," she agreed. "Really, Jess, you should find a better class of guy. Someone like Todd. He's dependable, trustworthy, loyal . . ." Elizabeth's voice trailed off as she listed her steady boyfriend's many great qualities.

Jessica stopped in front of a huge bulletin board covered with posters about everything going on at Sweet Valley High. She wrinkled her nose. In her opinion, Todd Wilkins was about as exciting as an algebra test. "Ugh.

That's not a boyfriend, that's a Boy Scout."

Mr. Collins, Sweet Valley High's most popular—not to mention most handsome—teacher, was pinning a turquoise-colored flier to the bulletin board. In addition to being an English teacher, Mr. Collins was the faculty advisor for Sweet Valley High's school newspaper, the *Oracle*. The flier he held announced auditions for an on-air version of the school paper.

Elizabeth ignored Jessica's not-so-flattering comment about Todd and smiled at her favorite teacher. "News show?" she asked, reading the flier. "What's the scoop, Mr. Collins?"

"The school's installing an in-class video system," Mr. Collins explained. "As of next week, the *Oracle* goes broadcast."

"Cool!" Elizabeth exclaimed. To Jessica's eternal bewilderment, her twin sister had a passion for journalism. Elizabeth often used her free time to investigate and write stories for the *Oracle*.

"Lame." Jessica rolled her eyes under the bill of her New York Yankees baseball cap. In her opinion, any news about the school newspaper was about as thrilling as, well, Todd Wilkins.

Elizabeth didn't seem to notice Jessica's lack of enthusiasm. Her eyes shone as she hugged the books she held. "What a great opportunity. I'm signing up now!"

As Elizabeth skipped into the *Oracle's* headquarters Jessica scanned the hallway. Much to her delight, a drop-dead-gorgeous stranger was heading her way. He held a television camera over one shoulder, and he looked distinctly more mature than the average Sweet Valley High guy. Once he'd passed, Jessica raised her eyebrows and smiled to herself. "Hello," she purred under her breath.

Jessica quickly followed the guy into the *Oracle* office. She ambled over to where the mystery man was taking some equipment from a cardboard box. Jessica stood still, waiting for him to take in her tight jersey T-shirt, fashionable suspenders, and cool baseball cap. She was sure it wouldn't take long for him to notice her.

"Can I help you?" he asked, still taking equipment from the box.

"You already have," Jessica replied, her voice sultry. She let her eyes roam over his longish dark blond hair, his great build, and his adorable smile.

"Russ Franklin," he said, his blue eyes holding hers. "I'm the video consultant for the news show."

"Oh, you're working on this?" she asked innocently, shaking Russ's hand. "I'm Jessica Wakefield—Sweet Valley High's next news anchor. Mind if I check out some of your equipment?"

Jessica couldn't have kept the flirtatious lilt out of her voice even if she'd wanted to. But behind Russ, she saw Elizabeth roll her eyes.

*   *   *

A little bit later, Jessica followed her new crush out of the *Oracle* office.

"So, you're a film major at Valley College, huh?" Jessica said as she walked with Russ into a makeshift TV studio. "Creative men really turn me on. That must be a really tough program."

"Oh, yeah, it's murder," Russ responded in an amused tone of voice. "We have to watch five movies a day—and get a load of this: they actually expect us to pay attention."

"*Brutal.*" Jessica couldn't imagine having to concentrate for such a long period of time.

"This is the nerve center of our operation," Russ said. He gestured toward the equipment that lined the room. "From here, I can put your face in every classroom in the school."

"Really? Awesome!" Jessica smiled at the idea of her gorgeous face being transmitted over the airwaves. She'd always wanted to be a famous actress. And the prospect of having instant fame *and* a relationship with Russ was making the on-air *Oracle* seem like a better and better plan. "You'd do that for me?" she asked Russ, treating him to her most seductive smile.

Russ nodded, handing Jessica a video camera and a tripod. "Yeah, I would. Of course, you have to put your audition tape together first. Mr. Collins has the final say."

Jessica gave Russ another long, smoldering

look. Suddenly she knew that she just *had* to get the anchor job.

Russ opened the studio door for Jessica, giving her an appreciative stare. "And don't worry about the camera," he said. "We're only supposed to loan it out for two days, but *you* can keep it as long as you want."

"Thanks. Let me know if there's ever *anything* I can do for you," Jessica said.

Russ grinned. "Good luck with your audition tape. I hope we'll be working together."

As Jessica watched Russ walk down the hallway, she didn't even feel the weight of the two tons of camera equipment piled in her arms.

"Count on it," she said aloud.

At lunchtime Elizabeth walked with Enid, Patty, and Lila to Sweet Valley High's outdoor tables. It was a beautiful day, and Elizabeth was bursting with excitement about the news show.

"What are you going to do for your audition tape, Liz?" Enid asked as the girls set down their trays.

"I'm not sure yet," Elizabeth responded. "Something with substance." She smiled into her best friend's twinkling eyes. She could always count on Enid for support.

"Well, I don't know about you guys, but I want to be the director," Patty said eagerly. "I mean, how hard could it be? I choreographed all our best cheers this year. I'm sure I could handle a little news show."

Patty was the captain of Sweet Valley High's cheerleading squad, and she was known for jumping into school activities with enthusiasm. Just as Elizabeth was about to ask Patty more about her directing ideas, her twin sister walked up behind them.

"Hello, future fans and news junkies," Jessica said. "Make room for Sweet Valley's new Barbara Walters." She sat down on the picnic bench, squeezing in between Elizabeth and Lila.

"Since when are you interested in journalism?" Elizabeth asked wryly.

"Journalism?" Jessica scoffed. "It's TV news!"

"Easy, Babs. You have to research and *write* your own stories." Elizabeth raised her eyebrows at her sister.

"Details, details," Jessica said, shrugging. "It's a small price to pay for having my face in every classroom."

On the other side of Sweet Valley High's lush courtyard, Winston Egbert was searching for a place to eat his lunch. A true class clown, Winston was everybody's friend—well, almost everybody's. He and Bruce Patman had been at odds with each other for quite a while. Winston couldn't stand the way rich and snobby Bruce thought he owned the world.

"Yo, Winston!" Bruce called from a nearby table, where he was sitting with his best friend, Manuel Lopez.

"What's up, Patman?" Winston said cautiously.

"Why so suspicious?" Bruce asked.

"Well, you called me Winston. What happened to Egghead, Eggbreath, Eggbeater, Eggnog, and Eggbrain?" Winston responded, listing all of Bruce's mean-spirited nicknames.

"Egg salad," Manuel added, holding up half of his sandwich.

"Good one, Manny," Bruce said, laughing. Then he turned to Winston. "You know, Winston, this thing between us is getting out of hand. I play a trick on you, you try to get me back. The anger we're building up could scar us for life." Bruce's voice sounded sincere. Winston looked at him with barely suppressed shock. Were his ears deceiving him?

"Here, let me get that," Bruce continued. He took Winston's tray and set it down on the table. "As I was saying, we should try to live together peacefully. Let bygones be bygones. Have a seat."

Winston sat down. "Have you suffered a severe trauma of the head recently, Bruce?"

"What a kidder, right, Manny? Truce." Bruce held out his hand, which Winston reluctantly shook. "This is nice. Can't you feel the love?"

Winston finally started to relax. It seemed that

Bruce was really trying to change. At that moment a beautiful girl walked by, giving the guys a little wave. Winston couldn't help staring—he would have given anything to go out with a girl like her.

"Whoa, Eggman. She wants you," Bruce said, gesturing toward the girl.

"You think?" Winston asked, his voice cracking.

"Yeah! Go talk to her!"

Winston decided to seize what might be the opportunity of a lifetime. But when he tried to get up, he realized he was stuck to the picnic bench.

"What's the matter, Egghead? Butt too heavy?" Bruce asked as Winston struggled to stand up. Then he pulled out a bottle of superglue. "Oh, gee, it's empty," he said, tossing the bottle into the air. "Someone must have spilled this all over the bench."

"Tough break, Eggplant," Manny said, his eyes sparkling.

Bruce and Manny walked away laughing, while Winston tried in vain to separate his pants from the picnic bench.

"I'll get you, Patman!" Winston yelled after his archenemy.

Just then Sweet Valley High's principal walked by. "Mr. Cooper," Winston greeted him weakly.

"Egbert! Stop that horseplay and get to class!" Mr. Cooper snapped.

Winston groaned. Not only was he humiliated—he was in trouble!

After school Elizabeth sat in the *Oracle* office, researching the stories she wanted to use for her audition tape. She was determined that every detail was going to be accurate.

"Can I quote you on that?" she said into the telephone she held. When the voice at the other end of the line agreed, Elizabeth smiled with satisfaction. "Thank you, Mr. Superintendent."

"Elizabeth, you're here late." Mr. Collins had walked into the office. She hung up the phone and gave him a grin.

"I'm just doing some fact-checking for my audition tape." she explained.

"I know you'll do a great job," Mr. Collins answered.

Elizabeth studied the notes she'd made. She silently agreed with Mr. Collins. She was *definitely* going to do a great job.

Scanning Sweet Valley High's parking lot to make sure that the coast was clear, Winston crept up to Bruce's black Porsche.

"You asked for it, Patman," he said under his breath, kneeling next to one of the Porsche's back tires. Quickly Winston began to let the air out of the tire. He couldn't wait to see Bruce's face when he realized that he had a flat. But just then he heard voices. Bruce and Manny were walking right toward Winston. In a flash, he took cover.

"Why do you want to get involved with this *Oracle* show, anyway?" Manny was asking Bruce.

"I want to do the editorials," Bruce said smugly. "Share my opinions. I feel I owe it to these simpletons to tell them how to think."

"Hey, you're the man," Manny responded.

"Of course." The guys slid into the sleek sports car.

"What about the audition tape?" Manny asked.

Bruce turned his key in the ignition. "It's a done deal. I made a call, and I'm bringing in the best director money can buy."

Bruce peeled out of the Sweet Valley High parking lot, and Winston sat up, coughing. He'd been lying flat on his back under Bruce's Porsche, and now he was covered with dirt and grease. His day was getting worse and worse. How was he ever going to get back at Bruce?

A few days later, Jessica and Elizabeth sat in the Wakefields' sunny living room. When Elizabeth's audition tape finished playing, she shut off the VCR and turned to her twin sister.

"So, what do you think?" Elizabeth asked, obviously pleased with the way her tape had turned out.

Jessica shrugged. "It's okay, I guess." Inside, Jessica was worried. Elizabeth's tape was a million times better than her own, which was nothing short of a TV disaster.

"Let's see yours," Elizabeth said brightly. She was still kneeling by the television set.

"I'd better not," Jessica said, thinking fast. She had no desire to listen to her twin tell her what a flop she was as an TV news anchor. "I wouldn't want to show you up."

"Since when?" Elizabeth asked archly.

"Trust me, Liz. I'm just trying to spare your feelings. I want you to be able to sleep tonight."

As Elizabeth shrugged and walked toward the stairs, Jessica stared at the blank TV screen. She was desperate to get the anchor job, and nothing was going to stand in her path. Not even her own sister.

Suddenly Jessica's eyes lit up. She glanced quickly around the living room, reassuring herself that her twin was nowhere in sight. Then Jessica stealthily switched the labels of her audition tape and Elizabeth's.

Jessica sat back on her heels, flipping her long blond hair over one shoulder. Sometimes being an identical twin had definite advantages!

The next afternoon, Mr. Collins and Russ Franklin sat in Sweet Valley High's TV studio, studying the dozens of audition tapes they'd received. At the moment, Bruce Patman was on the screen, winding up his editorial.

"And *that*, dear friends, is the Patman Perspective. For a transcript—" Even on television, Bruce's voice was arrogant.

"Talk about pompous," Russ said, shaking his head.

"Every news team needs a windbag," Mr. Collins commented. Then he reached for another of the audition tapes. "Ah, Elizabeth's tape. This should be good."

Russ pushed the VCR's play button, and Mr. Collins sat back to enjoy Elizabeth's fine work. But he realized almost immediately that *this* Elizabeth was not going to do the kind of great job he was used to.

"Hey there! Hello! Hi! Uh . . . hey, Sweet Valley," Elizabeth said on the tape. Her delivery was awkward, and she looked as if she cared more about smiling at the camera than reading the news.

"I can't believe it," Mr. Collins said, genuinely disappointed. "I was counting on her."

Russ leaned forward and grabbed another tape. "I've got someone with real potential," he said confidently. "Jessica Wakefield."

"*Jessica* Wakefield?" Mr. Collins asked doubtfully.

"She could carry your whole show. I'd stake my reputation on it." Russ popped the tape into the VCR.

A moment later, the two men listened to a mature and sophisticated young woman give Sweet Valley the daily news. "Good morning, Sweet Valley. Today's top story: after a recent probe into the school department's budget . . ."

Mr. Collins nodded at Russ. "Now there's our anchor," he said.

Just a short while later, Russ Franklin walked out of the studio with a list of the students who'd won on-air spots on the news show. The hall was crowded, and Elizabeth was so anxious to see whether she'd gotten the anchor position that she was practically hyperventilating.

"Hi, Russ," Elizabeth heard Jessica say as he tacked the list to the bulletin board. Russ winked at Jessica before he walked off down the hall.

Before anyone else could study the list, Bruce pushed his way to the front. "Editorial!" he yelled, punching his fist in the air. "The Pat-Man does it again! What's it feel like to be a *loser*, Eggward?" Bruce had turned to Winston and laughed in his face.

Before Winston could think of a snappy comeback, Bruce and Manny were gone. "There is no justice," Winston said dejectedly.

With Bruce gone, Jessica maneuvered her way toward the posted list. Elizabeth watched her sister's face brighten when she found her name.

"Yes! I got anchor!" Jessica yelled.

"I got the fashion forecast!" Lila squealed, standing right next to her. She smoothed her red hair. "Taste finally arrives at Sweet Valley High."

Elizabeth's heart sank. Seeing Lila on TV would be bad enough—almost as wealthy as Bruce Patman, Lila loved to flaunt her riches and be a snob. But *Jessica* as anchor . . . it was such a major blow that Elizabeth felt almost paralyzed with shock. She watched as Jessica sauntered a short way down the hall and tilted her head toward Russ's handsome face.

"So, Russ, it looks like we'll be working some long hours together," Jessica said.

"It'll be my pleasure."

"That's a start," Jessica responded.

Elizabeth rolled her eyes. She was completely sick of Jessica's constant flirting and her constant need to be the center of attention. The way she was acting with Russ was nothing short of embarrassing.

Elizabeth turned to her boyfriend, Todd, feeling in dire need of a sympathetic ear. "Jessica and Lila got on and I didn't? There must be some mistake."

Todd nodded. "Maybe you should talk to Mr. Collins."

Before Elizabeth could answer, Mr. Collins appeared at the door of the *Oracle* office. "OK, news team. Come get your story assignments."

"Go on," Todd said, jerking his head toward the teacher.

"I will," Elizabeth said, putting on a brave face. "Go get your assignment. I'll be fine." She forced her voice not to tremble as she spoke.

Todd leaned over and gave Elizabeth an affectionate kiss on the cheek. He had gotten an on-air position doing sports news, and Elizabeth watched as he went over to Mr. Collins to get his first assignment. Beside Todd, Elizabeth saw Jessica take the piece of paper Mr. Collins held out to her.

"You did an exceptional job, Jessica," Mr. Collins said warmly.

"I was good, wasn't I?" Jessica said, a big smile on her face.

Then Elizabeth watched her twin turn to Russ. "So, it looks like a tough assignment. Perhaps you could give me a hand . . . or maybe both hands."

Mr. Collins cleared his throat. "For those who didn't get on-air slots, there's still room on the crew. Talk to Patty."

Patty had gotten the position of director, and it seemed she was determined to take her new job seriously.

"I want everyone in the studio tomorrow morning by eight," she called out. "On-air staff, have your copy ready for Mr. Collins so he can approve it. We go live at nine."

At last Elizabeth was able to catch Mr. Collins's eye. "I thought my tape was really great," she said to him.

Mr. Collins smiled kindly. "Elizabeth, not everybody's meant to be an on-air personality. Some people, like yourself, excel at the written word." He walked back into the office. "There's still room on the crew," he added over his shoulder.

Elizabeth leaned back against the bulletin board, feeling as if the weight of the world were on her shoulders.

That evening Elizabeth sat at the counter of the Moon Beach Café, a popular Sweet Valley High hangout. The Moon Beach was an upscale diner, known for its great milk shakes and infamous Mega-burgers. Elizabeth sipped her diet soda, toying with the straw she held in her hand. Since finding out that Jessica had won the position of news anchor, Elizabeth's mood had gone steadily downhill.

In a booth behind her, Patty was meeting with the rest of the *Oracle* on-air crew. "I just don't see why you guys can't get it right," she heard Patty say irritably.

Todd's voice broke in on Elizabeth's thoughts. "Hey," he said gently, walking up behind her. He sat down on the stool next to hers and gave her a warm kiss on the lips.

"Hi," she answered, pushing her soda away.

"Man, Patty's really tripping on this director business," Todd commented, glancing at the booth behind them.

"People, *please!*" Patty said, rapping her knuckles on the tabletop.

"Are you feeling any better?" Todd asked, his voice concerned.

"Not really," Elizabeth answered.

"You're still the *Oracle's* star writer. No one can take that away from you."

Elizabeth knew her boyfriend was trying to make her feel better, but his efforts were in vain. "I wanted the job so badly, Todd. And I thought my work was really great."

"What did Collins say?"

"There's nothing he can do. If you ask me, they should change the name from *Oracle On Air* to *Airheads On Air*."

"Hey," Todd said. After all, he was one of the "airheads."

"Present company excluded, of course," Elizabeth said, allowing herself a tiny smile. Maybe she *was* overreacting a little.

At that moment Jessica walked into the Moon Beach Café with Russ Franklin. With her long hair swept up on her head and big hoop earrings in her ears, Jessica looked every inch a star.

"Hi, Liz," Jessica said cheerfully. Then she turned to Todd, who everyone knew was *not* one of Jessica's favorite people. "Hi, Todd," she added, an edge of sarcasm in her voice. "Have you guys met Russ?"

"Yes, I have," Elizabeth responded flatly.

Jessica gripped Russ's arm and leaned her head against his shoulder. "Well, I just wanted to say hi. Don't forget to watch me tomorrow."

As Russ and Jessica walked toward a booth, Elizabeth made a face. "Is it wrong to hate your sister with a passion?" she asked Todd.

"In this case, I think it's required," Todd said sympathetically.

Elizabeth stood up, glancing one last time at her sister. "I'd better get home. I feel a murder coming on."

Jessica slid into a booth next to Russ. Between getting her face in every classroom of Sweet Valley High and getting a romance going with Russ, her week was shaping up nicely.

The door to the Moon Beach Café flew open, and Lila Fowler breezed in. She was wearing a tight, long dress and a fashionable black beret. Over her arm she'd slung an expensive leather bag. Her eyes widened as she saw Russ sitting with Jessica. Lila and Jessica were fierce rivals as well as best friends, and whatever one had, the other wanted.

Lila reached the booth where Jessica and Russ sat and leaned on the back of the seat. "Hmmm. *College* man," Lila murmured appreciatively. "Hi, I'm Lila. Which Greek god are you?" She seemed to examine every bit of Russ's well-muscled arms, which were shown off by his form-fitting black tank top.

Jessica scowled at her friend. She wasn't in the mood for competition. She made sure that Lila could see the cozy way she was holding onto Russ's arm. "Lila, Russ and I are trying to talk here."

Lila leaned even closer, ignoring Jessica. "Russ, is it? Rrrrussss." She rolled the name off her tongue as if it were a fine piece of art to be pondered over and enjoyed. "Sounds kind of like an animal, doesn't it?"

Jessica raised her eyebrows at Russ, who seemed amused by Lila's tactics. "Your nose is shining," she told her best friend, hoping to distract Lila from her prey.

"It is? It is not. Is it? If you're lying . . ." Lila reached up and touched her nose, suddenly paranoid. "Back in a flash."

As Lila hurried toward the rest room to study herself in the mirror, Jessica decided it was time to go somewhere more private. "Let's bail before she comes back and ruptures a hormone," she suggested.

Jessica waved to her friends as she and Russ left the Moon Beach Café. Stepping out into the cool night air, she shivered with anticipation. She and Russ had a whole evening to look forward to—and with any luck at all, Lila would *not* find them again.

Meanwhile, Patty Gilbert was struggling to keep the attention of her crew. Her dark eyes were glowing with excitement as she discussed her ideas. Winston was trying to concentrate on her lecture about how *Oracle On Air* would be broadcast, but he'd just noticed Bruce walking into the Moon Beach Café. His mind immediately latched onto a possible way to get revenge on Bruce.

"I want a lot of close-ups," Patty was saying to the group. "Hello? Winston? Are you in this time zone?"

Winston looked from Bruce to Patty. "Hmmm? Oh, yeah. Zooms. Close-ups. Lots of energy." He started rising from the booth. "Gotta go now."

As Winston headed out of the restaurant he heard the others still talking. "Focus here, people. Focus," Patty was saying.

Winston laughed gleefully as he stepped out into the parking lot. As usual, Bruce had driven his sleek black Porsche, and the convertible top was down. Next to the car was a huge trash Dumpster. "Perfect," Winston said to himself. He jumped into the bin and picked up a bag full of garbage.

"Here's a little present for you, Trash-Man," he said, preparing to throw the bag into Bruce's car.

But before he could toss the trash bag, someone walked out of the restaurant. Winston ducked down in the Dumpster as the guy crossed the

Jessica's psyched to be Homecoming Queen.

Queen Elizabeth addresses her subjects.

Jessica flirts with danger. . . .

Whoops!

© Saban

Elizabeth's main squeeze.

The next Barbara Walters.

Lovely Lila.

"Can I quote you on that?"

Jessica always gets what she wants.

"The Patman Perspective."

Jessica was born to model.

The unveiling . . .

How could Jessica have done it?

"I'm in that painting, too."

A payback picnic.

Revenge is sweet.

Jessica needs a favor.

Dreaming of stardom.

© Saban

Jessica as Lady MacBeth.

Waiting for the reviews . . .

A limping Lila calls her doctor.

Jessica's juicy new role.

parking lot and hopped on his motorcycle, which was parked next to Bruce's Porsche. He didn't mind communing with a little garbage if it meant he'd finally get a chance to get the best of Bruce.

Winston listened as the guy started his motorcycle and sped out of the parking lot. Just to make sure he wasn't going to be discovered, Winston remained hidden for a few more moments. Then he took hold of the trash bag and threw it with all his might.

The bag flew into the air, and a second later Winston heard an outraged shout. But the shout didn't sound as if it had come from Bruce. In fact, the voice sounded suspiciously like . . . Mr. Cooper's.

Winston stood up in the Dumpster. In place of Bruce's Porsche was Mr. Cooper's silver convertible. And the older man was looking at Winston as if he'd like to bash him over the head.

"Can you believe these people don't separate their paper from their plastic?" Winston asked, trying to laugh.

"Egbert! Get down. Now!" The principal's voice left no room for argument.

"Just doing my part, uh, to save the environment," Winston said meekly. He sank back down into the garbage, groaning. Once again, his plan had backfired.

It was barely seven o'clock in the morning, and Elizabeth was sleeping peacefully, holding her teddy bear close. Suddenly her dream was interrupted by the sound of her twin's voice.

"Liz, wake up. You've gotta help me with my stories," Jessica said insistently.

Elizabeth opened her eyes and sat up. "Your stories? Don't tell me you didn't write them."

"Of course I wrote them. Okay, so maybe I didn't write them." Jessica knelt next to Elizabeth's bed and looked at her imploringly.

"Jess!" Elizabeth exclaimed, opening her eyes wide. She couldn't imagine being so irresponsible, although she supposed she shouldn't be surprised that Jessica had been.

"It's not my fault," Jessica said smoothly. She sat down on Elizabeth's bed, a pen and pad in her hand. "I didn't get in until three in the morning. We went to the movies."

"All night? What did you see?"

"I dunno, Russ was in the way. Liz, please. Here's the pen, I'm begging."

"Why can't you do it?" Elizabeth asked, getting more annoyed by the second.

"I have to put on my makeup," Jessica answered, as if she was being perfectly reasonable.

"You've got two hours!"

"I know, it'll be tight. But I can skip my bikini wax." Jessica smiled.

Elizabeth shook her head. "Sorry, Jess. It's your assignment. You'll have to do it yourself."

"Oh, I get it. You wanted the anchor job for

yourself, and this is your way of getting back at me. You'd let your own sister go down in flames just to satisfy your petty jealousy." Jessica's voice was hard and accusing.

"All right," Elizabeth finally agreed. She reluctantly took the pen and paper. "But this is the last time I bail you out."

"You're the greatest!" Jessica said happily. "And afterward I'll tell Collins you wrote the stories. He'll see how good you are, and he'll let you write all my stories. Me in front of the camera and you behind—we can be a team!"

Elizabeth flopped back against her yellow flowered pillowcases. How did Jessica always manage to get what she wanted?

Only two hours later, Elizabeth was perfectly groomed—wearing a pretty pink shirt and a flowered skirt—and had finished writing several great news stories.

Now she was in the *Oracle* office, printing out the stories from one of the school's computers. Suddenly her eyes fell on the VCR tape that was marked as Jessica's audition. Curious, Elizabeth took the tape from its case and rolled her chair toward the nearest television set.

But when she pushed the play button, she felt as if she'd been hit by lightning. Instead of seeing her sister onscreen, Elizabeth was staring at herself. In a flash, she realized that her devious twin had switched the audition tapes. Typical!

"Jessica!" Elizabeth said quietly, knitting her eyebrows. For once, Jessica was going to have to learn a lesson about ethics. No way was she getting away with this move. . . .

Outside Sweet Valley High's small broadcast studio, Jessica paced the hall nervously. She knew she looked beautiful in her short black dress and colorful T-shirt; her long hair flowed down her back, and her silver jewelry would look great on camera. But she needed to find Elizabeth and get the copy for her stories—fast!

"Have you seen Elizabeth?" she asked Winston, who was walking by with a pair of headphones on.

"Nope." Winston raced off, heading into the studio.

"Ten minutes, people!" Mr. Collins called, rushing down the hallway. "Jessica, I need to proof your copy."

Jessica bit her lip. "Sorry, Mr. C. Liz is still photocopying."

As Mr. Collins went into the studio Jessica heard Patty shouting instructions to the students operating the television cameras. "OK, looks good, camera one," Patty said into the microphone attached to her headset. "Camera two, zoom out . . . camera two? Hello, camera two?"

On the TV monitor, Patty saw that the operator of camera two had zoomed in on a very attractive female student.

"What is that, Manny?" Patty asked, clearly irritated.

"Oh, sorry," Manny said sheepishly, pulling back to a wider angle.

Just then Elizabeth appeared next to Jessica in the hallway.

"Where've you been? I need my stories!" Jessica said, her tone urgent.

Silently Elizabeth handed Jessica the sheaf of papers she held in her hand. Jessica looked at the sheets and her face fell. "These are blank!" she exclaimed.

Elizabeth smiled serenely. "They are? Silly me. I must've mixed up the stories I wrote with the ones you wrote."

"Is there some kind of irony here?" Jessica asked, frowning.

"Jess! How can you just stand there and pretend you don't know what I'm talking about?"

"I don't know. Practice?" Jessica said wryly.

"You knew how much I wanted to be anchor!" Elizabeth said, staring into Jessica's eyes. "And you switched tapes just so you could get the job. Or was it Russ you really wanted?"

"Thirty seconds!" Jessica heard Patty call to the crew. "Where's Jessica?"

"Okay, okay. I admit it," Jessica said to her twin. By now she was desperate enough to apologize. "I was dishonest, selfish, and wrong. Can I please just have the stories?"

"Fifteen seconds!" she heard Patty yell. Jessica gave her sister a pleading look, but Elizabeth just folded her arms and stared back stubbornly.

"Jessica, you're on *now!*" Mr. Collins said, sticking his head out of the door of the studio.

"But the stories—" Jessica started to say.

"No time to proof them," Mr. Collins interrupted. "I'll just have to trust you. Now go! We're *live*, remember?"

"Four, three, two . . ." Patty's voice counted down the seconds until the live broadcast was to start.

Just as Patty ended the countdown, Jessica slid into the chair behind the anchor's desk. Over her head was a sign that read ORACLE ON AIR. Jessica took a deep breath, praying that she could pull off the broadcast with no major disasters.

"Hello. I'm Jessica Fakewield—Wakefield—with the *Oracle On Air* news," Jessica began, realizing that so far she sounded like an utter fool. "So . . . Here we are. Our first live broadcast," she improvised.

Through the glass window of the studio, she saw Mr. Collins gesturing for her to speed up and get to the news stories. Jessica gulped.

"Oh! The news. Yeah, well, a lot has happened this week. Bunches . . ." Jessica's voice faltered, and she suddenly knew that there was absolutely no way she could finish the broadcast. Without Elizabeth's stories, she was sunk. Mustering as much dignity as she could, Jessica decided to take an extreme measure. "And now, with the details of today's news, here's my sister, Elizabeth," Jessica said, mentally willing her twin to step up to the anchor desk. "Elizabeth?"

Out in the hallway, Mr. Collins shook his head and turned to Elizabeth, who stood beside him. "I should have known," he said. Go get 'em, Liz."

Grinning, Elizabeth walked into the room where Jessica sat at the anchor's desk. "Thank you, Jessica," she said.

"Anytime," Jessica answered. As quickly as she could, she got out of her chair and skulked into the hallway.

Elizabeth took her sister's place, holding her typed stories before her. "Good morning, Sweet Valley. I'm Elizabeth Wakefield with the news you need to know. Today's top stories . . ."

As Elizabeth's melodious voice read the news, Mr. Collins pulled Jessica aside in the hallway. "We should talk," he said sternly.

Jessica swallowed hard. Once again she'd landed herself in major hot water.

Patty leaned over the studio's control panel, watching Elizabeth with satisfaction. The broadcast was finally coming together.

"Winston, it still says 'Jessica,'" Patty said,

referring to the name that ran at the bottom of the screen. "Type in a new one for Elizabeth."

"You got it," Winston answered, punching letters into the keyboard at his fingertips.

The whole crew listened as Elizabeth continued the smooth flow of her story. "After discussion with the superintendent of schools, this money will now be redirected to the Sweet Valley High Activities Committee," she said, her voice coming through the audio equipment loud and clear.

"Perfect," Patty said as Elizabeth's name showed up on the screen. "You're up next, Bruce."

At the sound of Bruce's name, Winston growled. The thought of having to listen to Bruce spout his idiotic editorial was making Winston feel sick to his stomach. "Bruce," he muttered under his breath.

"That's all the news you need to know. Till next time, Sweet Valley," Winston heard Elizabeth say, concluding the news portion of the show. "And now, with his *unique* take on Sweet Valley, Bruce Patman."

Elizabeth stood up, and Bruce materialized behind her. On the wall behind the desk, he tacked a poster of himself, with "Patman Perspective" printed along one side. Then Bruce took his chair, looking supremely confident. "Thank you, Jess—I mean Elizabeth," Bruce said, glancing at Elizabeth. "Hello, fellow Gladiators.

As if you didn't know, I'm Bruce Patman. And this is the Patman Perspective."

In the studio, Patty looked over at Winston. "Why isn't Bruce's name on-screen?" she asked anxiously.

"Coming right up!" Winston said, excitedly typing on the keyboard. He couldn't help chuckling a little.

When Winston finished typing and pressed enter, text began scrolling under Bruce's face. "See how my nostrils flare when I talk?" it read.

Patty groaned, but she couldn't help laughing. Bruce had no idea that those words were appearing on-screen. Patty went over to Winston and playfully tried to strangle him. "Winston!"

Winston laughed. His revenge was just beginning. He studied the television monitor, where Bruce was continuing his editorial.

"It's popular today to attack the rich," Bruce said dramatically. "Now, I'm not obsessed with money, but I say there's nothing wrong with having it. I love the way it feels. I love the way it smells. I love what money does for me. I never go anywhere without my money."

As Bruce spoke he picked up stacks of dollar bills and held them up to the camera. The adoration he felt for cold, hard cash was written all over his face. But Bruce didn't know that Winston had struck again.

While Bruce went on and on about his love for money, Winston had typed in a new message for the viewers of *Oracle On Air:* "Money is the name of my gerbil" was printed in block letters across the screen.

"I have more money than money can buy. It's the best thing next to my Porsche. . . ."

As Bruce finished up his piece Winston—and everybody else—collapsed with laughter. The mighty Pat-Man had finally gotten what he deserved!

Jessica sighed, watching Mr. Collins's back retreat into the studio. He wasn't happy with her—far from it. Now Jessica had to go confess to the principal. She could just imagine how many hours of detention this little prank would merit. She leaned against the wall, shaking her head despondently.

"What did Collins say?" Elizabeth asked, coming down the hall. She stopped in front of her twin.

"I have to talk to Mr. Cooper."

Elizabeth shrugged. "You can't say you don't deserve it."

Jessica regarded her sister. Sometimes Elizabeth could really be devious—a quality Jessica had always admired in a person. "Hey, nice move back there," Jessica said, her voice conciliatory. "You really got me."

"Yeah, I did, didn't I?" Elizabeth grinned, swinging her long braid over one shoulder.

"I'm impressed," Jessica said with new respect for her twin.

"You're a nightmare," Elizabeth responded. But Jessica could hear the love in her sister's voice. Their battle was over.

As Elizabeth disappeared into the studio Jessica realized that despite getting her in trouble, her ethically questionable methods had also gotten her one very important thing: Russ Franklin.

After the first live broadcast of *Oracle On Air*, Bruce strolled down the hall of Sweet Valley High. He knew he'd done a great job—not that there had been any doubt about his skill and talent. Since he'd finished his editorial, almost every student he'd seen had smiled at him. Being in the spotlight felt awesome.

Suddenly Manuel barreled through one of Sweet Valley High's heavy doors. When he saw Bruce he came over to him and gave him a friendly slap on the back.

"Oh, man, Bruce," Manny said enthusiastically. "You were great today! Those jokes running under your editorial were a howl!"

"Jokes?" Bruce asked, confused. He had no idea what Manny was talking about, but he had a sinking feeling that he wasn't going to like the answer.

"Don't be so modest. Money's the name of your gerbil?" Manny laughed. "That's funny stuff!"

A light bulb went on in Bruce's mind. And when he caught sight of Winston Egbert and Enid Rollins, who were giggling next to Enid's locker, he got a crystal-clear picture of what had happened.

When Winston realized that Bruce was staring at him, his eyes widened, and he took off down the hallway. It looked as if the war was still on.

"Egbert!" Bruce shouted, racing after him. "I'll get you!"

Elizabeth stood in the doorway of a classroom, watching Jessica go into action as Russ Franklin emerged from the *Oracle On Air* studio. Even Elizabeth had noticed how gorgeous Russ looked that morning. Wearing a crisp white shirt and a beige linen vest, he was stylish, muscular, and classically good-looking, all rolled into one.

"Russ, now that I'm going to have more free time, what do you say we spend it together?" Jessica said provocatively. She wrapped her arms around Russ's waist and leaned close.

"I don't think so," Russ answered shortly. He untangled himself from Jessica and stepped backward.

Jessica immediately began to pout. It was a look that Elizabeth had seen a thousand times before. "What's the matter?" she asked Russ.

"Jessica, you made a fool of yourself and a fool of me," Russ said, raising his eyebrows. "Now if you'll excuse me . . ."

Russ walked off, his head held high. Elizabeth watched Jessica's shoulders droop. Her twin hated rejection.

When Jessica realized that Elizabeth was within earshot, she stood up straight, obviously trying to regain her dignity.

"And don't call me. I'll call you," Jessica yelled, pretending that she hadn't seen her twin standing close by. "Film geek," she added for good measure.

Elizabeth didn't bother to say anything. Jessica had suffered enough humiliation for one day.

At that moment one of the more attractive male members of the *Oracle On Air* crew walked out of the studio. Elizabeth saw her twin's eyes light up.

"Hey, Rob. Wait up," Jessica called. She tossed her long hair and set off in pursuit of her newest distraction.

Elizabeth shook her head, grinning. Poor Rob didn't stand a chance. Her twin sister was definitely one of a kind. *Thank goodness for that!* Elizabeth thought.

Still, Elizabeth wouldn't have traded Jessica for anyone—her twin had a way of making life into one big adventure. And even conservative Elizabeth loved adventure!

SKIN AND BONES

Based on the teleplay by Lanny Horn

Jessica Wakefield, Patty Gilbert, and Lila Fowler stood looking at Sweet Valley High's "graffiti wall." The wall was a place where students could display any of the work they'd done—including funny pictures, stories, and photographs.

At the moment, the girls were laughing at a photograph of the principal, Mr. Cooper, that Winston Egbert had taken. Because Sweet Valley High's principal was almost completely bald, the students had nicknamed him Chrome Dome. In Winston's photo, Chrome Dome was dabbing his bald head with a handkerchief, and the dissatisfied expression on his face was enough to make anyone laugh out loud.

Both Jessica and Patty were wearing their red and white cheerleading uniforms, and Lila was dressed as impeccably as always. Jessica was secretly pining after Lila's brown suede jacket, but she wasn't about to tell her best friend that she was jealous. Instead, Jessica focused on the graffiti wall.

"'Not only am I the president of the Hair Team for Men, I'm also its biggest failure,'" Jessica read aloud from the caption above the principal's head.

"Mr. Cooper's gonna freak," Patty commented, giggling.

"It's one of Winston's best jokes," Lila agreed.

"Well, well, well, what do I see?" Jessica said, staring at someone down the hall.

In the distance, she had spotted tall and lean Dakota Dancer. He was known throughout the high school for both his bad-boy good looks and his status as Sweet Valley's number-one young artist.

"Dakota Dancer is so hot," Patty said, taking the words right out of Jessica's mouth.

"Tell me about it," she agreed.

"I love the brooding artistic type," Patty sighed.

"So what is he doing with Enid?" Jessica asked, wrinkling her nose with distaste at the sight of her sister's best friend.

In Jessica's opinion, Enid Rollins was boring with a capital *B*. Jessica could never understand why Elizabeth hung out with her so much. After all, Enid wasn't nearly as pretty as Jessica—or even as pretty as Lila and Patty.

"Haven't you heard? She's his new model," Lila told Jessica, gesturing down the hall toward Enid and Dakota.

"No way. What would the best artist in Sweet Valley want with her?" Jessica said. At the word *model*, Jessica had suddenly become interested in Enid.

"Apparently she's his inspiration," Lila answered, eyeing Enid critically.

Jessica watched as the mismatched couple walked toward them. Enid was smiling up at Dakota, and even Jessica had to admit that being a model seemed to agree with her. She was wearing a very hip dress, and she had her long hair in two cute braids. Seeing Enid look so pretty made Jessica doubly anxious to wheedle her way into Dakota Dancer's life—and get Enid out of it.

"Hi, guys," Enid said as soon as she and Dakota got close to the group of ogling girls. Enid's voice was dreamy, and she gazed constantly into Dakota's eyes.

"Couldn't you just gag?" Lila said as soon as they had passed. "Can you imagine her in his `Spirit of Sweet Valley' painting?"

"She's got the spirit of a *sponge*. Dakota could do so much better," Jessica said. "He needs a more inspiring model."

"And I'm sure you have just the person in mind," Lila said. She knew exactly how Jessica's brain worked.

"Give me a *J*, give me an *E*—" Jessica sang, as if she were cheering.

"Give me a break," Patty interrupted.

"You're too late, Jess," Lila agreed. "That painting has to be finished for the art show on Friday, and then it goes on national tour."

"National tour? That's unreal. Dakota's gonna make Enid famous," Patty said.

Jessica narrowed her eyes, but said nothing. She had a plan—and it didn't include Dakota Dancer's making Enid famous.

Todd and Elizabeth strolled down the hallway of Sweet Valley High, hand in hand. Ever since their recent temporary breakup, they had been closer than ever. As they passed a bank of lockers Todd pulled Elizabeth into a small, semiprivate alcove. Then he stepped close to her and kissed her warmly.

"Todd," Elizabeth said playfully, gently pushing him away.

"What?" he asked, leaning forward to kiss her again.

Suddenly a flashbulb went off in their faces. Elizabeth heard the click of a camera and Winston's laughter.

"*That*," Elizabeth said, pointing at Winston and his ever-present camera.

"Copies will go on sale in the student store," Winston said, smiling at them.

"Winston, chill with the pictures, huh?" Todd said. Although Winston and Todd were best friends, they didn't always share the same sense of humor.

"You'll be begging me to snap more when you see who's made the graffiti wall this week," Winston said.

Todd, Elizabeth, and Winston walked toward the graffiti wall, where Bruce and Manuel were laughing at the picture of Mr. Cooper.

"Old Chrome Dome never looked better," Bruce said.

"Oooh, the glare," Manny answered, slipping on a pair of sunglasses. "I wonder if he waxes that thing."

Bruce raised an eyebrow and stared over his friend's head. Manny frowned. "He's behind me, isn't he?" Manny said, grimacing.

Bruce nodded. "Say, Mr. Cooper, I see Winston's done it to you again," he joked.

"Looks like," the principal responded flatly. Then he walked up to the embarrassing photograph and pulled it off the wall.

"You can't do that," Winston protested. He, Elizabeth, and Todd had been watching the scene from a short distance away.

"I thought we could put anything on the graffiti wall," Elizabeth said to the principal.

"I draw the line on personal attacks," Mr. Cooper answered angrily. His face was slightly red, and there was a glistening of sweat on his bald head.

"Isn't that censorship?" Todd asked.

"Whatever happened to freedom of expression?" Elizabeth added, frustrated with Mr. Cooper's attitude.

"It's still here. Just the picture isn't," Mr. Cooper said. Then he walked off toward his office, clutching the photograph as if he was afraid that someone would try to grab it.

"And that was some of my best work," Winston complained forlornly.

"He can't do that, can he?" Todd asked Elizabeth.

Elizabeth stared in the direction that Mr. Cooper had gone. "Not if I can help it," she said, her voice hard and determined.

Jessica walked into the art room where she knew Dakota Dancer worked on most of his projects. The room was cluttered with paint cans, drop cloths, easels, and paintbrushes. Loud music played from a portable stereo, and Dakota was studying the composition of a painting on the easel in front of him. Jessica shut the door behind her and fixed a steady gaze on Dakota. She reached over and turned off the music.

Dakota's long hair was loose and messy, and he looked particularly appealing. But he didn't appear overjoyed to have been interrupted. "What?" he asked.

"I heard you're looking for a new model," Jessica said. She struck a pose, allowing Dakota to absorb how great she looked in her short cheerleading uniform.

"Position's filled," he said shortly. He barely bothered to glance at her.

"But I admire your work so much," Jessica said, moving toward him. "I'd really like to see you in action . . . creating." She took another step toward him. "Creative people are so . . . creative."

"You want to work with me?" he asked, dipping a small brush into the white paint on his palette.

"More than you can possibly imagine," Jessica whispered. She realized she was making progress, and she felt a flutter of excitement.

He shrugged. "Clean these," he said, passing her a handful of paintbrushes. He immediately turned back to the easel.

"Yuck," Jessica said, staring at the brushes. Being a maid wasn't exactly what she had in mind. But she went over to the sink in the corner, sure that Dakota would eventually see things her way. As she reached for the faucet the door opened. Jessica stepped behind the door so that she could observe whatever was about to happen.

"Hi, Dakota," Enid said shyly. She walked over to the artist and stared at his canvas.

"Enid," Dakota said, his voice friendly.

"Oh, wow, that's . . . amazing. I mean, it's

going to be amazing when you're finished," Enid said. She looked at him, admiration shining in her eyes.

"That's a color test," Dakota answered matter-of-factly.

"I knew that," Enid said quickly.

Jessica had had enough. She slammed the art room door shut, causing Enid to jump in surprise. "What are *you* doing here?" Enid gasped.

"I'm Dakota's new personal assistant," Jessica answered, hoping that Enid would become intimidated and go away.

"Oh." Enid sounded disappointed.

Dakota looked at Enid. "About tomorrow—the beach. Noon."

"I'll be there," Enid said eagerly. "Anything else?"

"Dress comfortably."

"Sure, okay. See you there." Enid glanced at Jessica one last time, then walked out of the room.

Once she was gone, Jessica stared at Dakota. A sly smile spread across her face as she formulated one of her brilliant plans. . . .

After school, Jessica rushed into the Moon Beach Café. As soon as she put her plan into motion, she would be on her way to becoming a famous model.

"Enid, there you are," Jessica said, approaching a booth were Enid was drinking a vanilla milk shake. "I'm so glad I found you."

"Oh, yeah, sure," Enid responded sarcastically. She took a sip of her milk shake without bothering to look at Jessica.

"No, really, I want to do you a favor."

"Since when?" Enid asked. She knew as well as anyone else that Jessica rarely did anyone a favor.

"Since you're my sister's best friend," Jessica said, her voice innocent. "Look, I hate to tell you this, but you can't be the model for Dakota's painting."

Enid glared at her. "I knew it. You're jealous." She turned back to her milk shake.

"Jealous? Of you?" Jessica scoffed. "Enid, don't forget who you're talking to."

"I'm not," Enid said emphatically. "You can't stand it that Dakota's painting *me* and not you."

"Okay. Fine. But don't say I didn't try to warn you!" Jessica sped out of the Moon Beach as if she couldn't care less whether or not Enid took her advice.

Outside, Jessica climbed into the Jeep, tossing aside her pom-poms. Just as she was anticipating, Enid came barreling out after her.

"Warn me about what?" she asked, running up to Jessica.

Jessica gave Enid a condescending smile. "Oh, just that Dakota's planning to paint you nude."

"Nude?" Enid asked, incredulous.

"As in naked. Without clothing. *Au naturel*."

"You're crazy," Enid insisted. "Why did he tell me to wear comfortable clothes?"

"So you could slip out of them more easily," Jessica said, as if Dakota's intentions were the most obvious thing in the world.

"But I thought he really wanted to paint me." Enid's voice was a combination of sadness and anger.

"Oh, he does . . . *all* of you." Jessica grinned. Her plan was going exactly as she'd wanted it to.

"That total pig," Enid yelled. "I'm gonna tell him off." She started to leave, but Jessica grabbed her arm.

"Wait, Enid. Let me. I've got a lot more experience with jerks like Dakota Dancer," Jessica said kindly.

"Thanks, Jess," Enid said, looking relieved. "I guess I misjudged you."

"Oh, don't be too hard on yourself," Jessica said. She turned on the ignition and pulled out of the Moon Beach Café's parking lot with a self-satisfied smile. Poor Enid hadn't had any idea what she was up against.

The next morning Elizabeth sat in the *Oracle* office, surveying her latest editorial. Todd was reading the paper as he stood in the doorway. The front page was splashed with a headline that

Elizabeth hoped would inflame the students and make Mr. Cooper rethink his position: "Save the Graffiti Wall. Cooper, No Principles!"

"'Cooper, No Principles'?" Todd read aloud. "Way to go, Liz. Chrome Dome is gonna blow his lid."

"He deserves it," Elizabeth answered. After she saw Mr. Cooper take down the photograph of himself, she had written a last-minute editorial about the evils of censorship.

"Uh-oh. Speak of the Dome," Todd said.

Elizabeth stood up so she could peer down the hallway. "What's he going to do? Shut down the *Oracle?*" she asked her boyfriend. Then she shuddered. At that point, she wouldn't be surprised by anything Mr. Cooper tried to do.

"Good luck," Todd said. He kissed her, then slipped out of the office.

"Ms. Wakefield. May I have a word?" Mr. Cooper's tone was stern, and he looked as if he were about to breathe fire. He slapped a copy of the *Oracle* onto the table next to Elizabeth. "Care to explain?"

"Just standing up for students' rights," Elizabeth said, her voice strong and calm.

"Humiliating the faculty is not my idea of creative expression," he said.

"If the students want to put up funny pictures of people, they're entitled. It's not your call." Elizabeth was passionate about the right to free

78

speech, and she wasn't about to back down on her position.

"There is a fine line between expression and good taste," Mr. Cooper said. "When I gave the students the graffiti wall, I entrusted them to govern themselves. If they can't do that, then it is up to me to offer guidance."

"What you did isn't guidance. It's censorship." Elizabeth stared Mr. Cooper in the eye, silently challenging him to try to tell her otherwise.

Just before noon, Jessica jumped out of the Jeep and grabbed her beach bag. She could see that Dakota had set up his easel next to a small lake with a sandy beach at one end of it. The spot was beautiful and peaceful; Jessica could hear birds singing in the trees. She always loved being away from school in the middle of the day, and today she had been excused from afternoon classes in order to work for Dakota. She practically felt like singing. She couldn't wait for Dakota to make her famous.

"What are you doing?" Dakota asked when she appeared before him. He was standing in front of an easel and was already busy painting. He didn't sound pleased to see her.

"What any good assistant would do," Jessica said sweetly. "I got here as soon as I could. It's Enid. She totally flaked."

"In English, please," Dakota said, apparently

not appreciating Jessica's description.

"Enid's not coming," Jessica explained. "I didn't want to let you down, so I called everyone else I knew. Nobody could make it."

"I need a model," Dakota fumed. For the first time he glanced away from his canvas.

"That's what I figured," Jessica said, walking toward a tree. "So . . ." Jessica unzipped her short black dress and revealed her skimpiest leopard-print bikini.

"How's this?" she asked huskily. She let her dress fall to the ground and began posing for Dakota. There was no way he could resist painting her.

Jessica positioned her body several different ways, but Dakota kept shaking his head. After a few minutes, Jessica sighed with frustration. She knew she looked beautiful, and she thought Dakota should be happy to paint her in *any* pose.

Finally Dakota pointed to the ground next to the tree. "Over there," he said.

Jessica lounged on the ground, trying to get comfortable and look alluring at the same time. Again Dakota shook his head.

He set down his paintbrush and walked over to Jessica. He used his hands to tilt up her chin, then indicated how she should position the rest of her body. "Hold it right there!" he commanded.

"Are you sure you don't want to see it another way?" Jessica asked. The ground under her was hard, and she could tell that it wasn't going to take long for her muscles to get stiff.

Instead of answering, Dakota just started painting. Jessica gritted her teeth and smiled, determined to be the best model he'd ever had.

Back at Sweet Valley High, Winston was prowling the halls with his camera in hand. He liked to use every free minute to try to find fellow students in embarrassing situations. Bruce Patman was one of his favorite targets.

Winston sneaked around a corner near Bruce's locker, hiding behind an open classroom door. When he peeked out, he could see Bruce standing in front of his locker. There was a full-length mirror attached to the inside of the locker door, and Bruce was studying his reflection and preening. After a moment, he cast a furtive glance around the hall, then struck a muscle-man pose. He stared at himself, grinning.

Winston seized his opportunity and crept up behind Bruce. Then he snapped a quick picture. Bruce wheeled around, a look of fury in his eyes. "Pray I don't catch you, Eggbrain!" Bruce shouted.

Winston tore down the hall, Bruce close on his heels. He couldn't wait to get his latest photo onto the graffiti wall.

Hours later, Jessica zipped up her black dress. Dakota had finished the painting and now he was packing up his equipment. Jessica walked toward him, relieved to be able to move again. She'd been distinctly uncomfortable for what had seemed like forever.

"How does Cindy Crawford do this?" she asked Dakota, who was sliding his painting into a specially designed wooden box. When he didn't bother to answer, Jessica glanced at the edge of the canvas. "Can I see it?" she asked.

"Tomorrow. At the unveiling." Dakota lifted up the box and headed for his car.

Watching him, Jessica realized that he hadn't even bothered to thank her. Dakota was gorgeous and sexy, but he wasn't exactly a gentleman.

Late that afternoon Jessica, Elizabeth, Lila, and Patty strolled through the Valley Mall, drinking sodas and window-shopping. Elizabeth was still angry about her encounter with Mr. Cooper, and she told the others about the incident as they walked.

"Cooper totally avoided the issue," Elizabeth said, waving around her soda cup for emphasis. "It's censorship plain and simple."

Jessica was admiring her reflection in the windows of the stores they were passing. In jean shorts and a button-down blouse knotted at her waist, Jessica was stunning. She had no doubt that as soon as everyone saw her in Dakota's painting, every modeling agency in town would be hounding her.

"Yeah, yeah, whatever," Jessica said, bored with the whole subject of censorship. "The world doesn't revolve around the *Oracle* and that stupid graffiti wall. Other people have lives, too, you know." She paused briefly. "Anybody going to the art opening tomorrow?"

"Everybody who's anybody will be there," Lila said. "I bet Enid's so psyched."

"Enid?" Jessica asked, turning to look at her best friend. "Lila, I thought you of all people would have heard."

"Heard what?" Lila responded, her voice suspicious.

"Enid is out of the picture." Jessica smiled, pleased to see the shock registering on her friends' faces.

"Don't tell me," Lila said, shaking her head.

"What can I say? Dakota saw what he wanted and he was inspired, if you know what I mean."

"Oh, Jess, you didn't," Elizabeth exclaimed, a look of alarm crossing her pretty face. She knew how much being Dakota's model had meant to Enid.

"You were his model?" Patty asked, sighing. "How was it?"

"Put it this way: the beach, me, coconut oil, Dakota. Let's just say the waves were crashing."

"Sounds hot," Lila commented. She tossed her paper cup into the trash can and stared enviously at Jessica.

"Your curling iron hasn't seen this kind of heat," Jessica responded.

Friday evening Elizabeth and Todd walked into Dakota Dancer's art opening. Although Elizabeth sympathized with Enid's having lost her position as Dakota's model, she was excited for Jessica. She and Todd stopped next to a painting that was draped with a red velvet cloth and gold-colored rope.

"Just think, in three weeks people all over the country will see Jessica's face," Elizabeth said to Todd, glancing at the veiled painting.

"Yours too. In a way," he answered, leaning over and kissing Elizabeth's cheek.

As Elizabeth and Todd gazed into each other's eyes, Patty appeared at their side. "Where's Enid?" she asked Elizabeth.

"I don't know," Elizabeth responded, her voice concerned. "She left this weird message on my machine. Something about boycotting anything Dakota does."

Patty raised her eyebrows and shrugged, but Elizabeth's heart went out to Enid. Obviously her best friend was hurt. Elizabeth just hoped that Enid would get over it quickly.

On the other side of the room, Jessica and Lila stood near the refreshment table. Jessica surveyed the room, relishing the fact that soon everyone's eyes would be on her.

"What a turnout. And to think they're all here because of me," Jessica said to Lila.

"Reality check. They're all here because of *Dakota*," Lila replied. Lila and Jessica were always competitive, and Lila was always quick to point out when her friend's ego was overinflated.

"Come on, great art is known by its inspiration—Venus de Milo, Mona Lisa, and now me." Jessica wasn't about to let Lila's attitude take away from her moment in the limelight.

"Please," Lila snorted.

"I've prepared a few words," Jessica continued. She was determined to ignore Lila's lack of enthusiasm.

"You're not making a speech, are you?" Lila's voice was edged with disbelief.

"Trust me, when they see the painting, they'll be *begging* for one," Jessica said confidently.

Suddenly Winston and his camera were in Jessica's face. "Smile!" Winston called.

Jessica posed for the camera, then turned to Lila. "See? It's already starting."

Mr. Cooper moved to the front of the room and stood next to the easel on which Dakota's covered painting was propped. "Good evening, everyone. On behalf of Sweet Valley High, I'd like to thank you all for coming to this grand event."

There was light applause, and Mr. Cooper smiled at some of the adults who were milling about the room. "Tonight we'll be unveiling the most recent work of Dakota Dancer," he continued.

Standing next to Mr. Cooper, Dakota smiled broadly. The short sleeves of his white T-shirt revealed several tattoos, and his long dark hair was mussed attractively around his face. Jessica thought he was one of the most dangerously attractive guys she'd ever seen.

"I shall always look back on this night as a high point in the school's history," the principal said, his voice booming through the room. "Now, without any further ado, I give you an *artiste extraordinaire*, Dakota Dancer."

Dakota acknowledged Mr. Cooper with a nod, then moved to the spot where the principal had been giving his speech. The room quieted down as everyone settled in to listen to Dakota's words about his latest work.

"'The Spirit of Sweet Valley' could never have been painted without a woman who gave her all for this vision," Dakota said, looking straight at Jessica. "Jessica Wakefield." He gestured toward her, and she smiled.

"Thank you, Dakota. You've captured a side of me that few people have ever seen." Jessica glanced around the room so that everyone could get a good look at the flesh and blood behind the art. Wearing a fashionable suit and with her hair swept up on top of her head, Jessica felt beautiful and sophisticated.

Dakota pulled the gold-colored cord that was attached to the red drape, dramatically revealing the painting that everyone had gathered to view. Immediately the room was filled with the sound of a collective gasp.

Jessica's jaw dropped, and tears sprang to her eyes. Next to her, Lila's eyes widened, and she giggled. Patty had a shocked expression on her face.

"She's naked!" Elizabeth exclaimed. She couldn't believe her sister had agreed to pose nude. Even Jessica seemed incapable of a stunt like this. Did she really need attention that badly?

"Bravo!" Bruce yelled, clapping.

As some of the other guys joined in, cheering, Winston snapped several pictures. Jessica helplessly watched the flash of Winston's camera, and for once in her life she was speechless.

In the Moon Beach Café, Manny and Bruce sat in a booth. "I never knew how cool art could be," Bruce said to Manuel. "You know, I think I may start collecting."

Manny grinned, and the two boys gave each other a high five.

Across the diner, Enid, Patty, and Lila sat at the counter. Patty and Lila had filled Enid in on the events of the art show, and Enid was incredulous that Jessica had gone through with modeling for Dakota.

"There's no way I'd ever pose nude," Enid said, shaking her head. "I can't believe she actually did it."

"It doesn't surprise me at all. Jessica would do anything for attention," Lila sniffed.

"She has no shame," Patty agreed.

"Yeah. Did you notice there weren't any tan lines?" Lila said cattily.

The girls giggled, then fell silent as Jessica walked into the Moon Beach. Instantly the guys in the diner started to clap and whistle.

"Jessica, beautiful portrait," Bruce called to her. "I wasn't aware of such hidden talents."

"You think it was anatomically correct?" Manny asked Bruce, eyeing Jessica as she walked over to the counter.

"Hey, Jessica, wanna go out sometime? I've got some finger paints," once leering guy yelled.

Jessica continued to walk toward her friends, determinedly keeping her head held high. She cast scathing glances at the guys who were making fun of her, but she refused to dignify their remarks with a comment.

Elizabeth came into the Moon Beach behind Jessica, and she headed toward Todd, who was waiting for her at one end of the long counter.

"They're dissing her big-time," Todd informed her.

Elizabeth shook her head sadly. Jessica had

really made a fool of herself, and no one was going to let her forget it.

By the time Jessica reached her friends, she was badly in need of some support. "How can they believe I would pose nude?" she asked Patty, Enid, and Lila. They all stared in another direction, refusing to meet her eyes.

"Well, you guys believe me, don't you?" Jessica asked, her voice desperate. "I was wearing a bathing suit, okay? Dakota did the rest on his own." She sat back, waiting for them to apologize.

"How dumb do you think we are?" Enid yelled. "You're the one who said Dakota wanted to do a nude. Quit lying." Without another word, Enid stormed away from the counter.

Patty glanced over at Jessica, who was sitting with her arms crossed defiantly. "Jessica, how about the truth? You're the one who told us about the beach, the suntan oil—"

"The waves, crashing," Lila interjected, raising her eyebrows.

"Or were you lying about that?" Patty asked.

"You don't understand. . . ." Jessica's voice trailed off. She felt completely helpless.

"I think I do," Patty said, sounding disgusted. She got up from her stool, obviously having nothing more to say to Jessica.

Once Patty was gone, Lila turned to Jessica. "Come on," she said in a confidential tone. "I'm your best friend. You can tell me the truth."

"I am!" Jessica insisted. She didn't know how to be any more clear about the fact that Dakota had misrepresented her in that horrible painting.

"Everyone knows you'd have done anything to get Dakota," Lila pointed out. "Why don't you just admit it?"

Lila stood up, leaving Jessica sitting all alone at the counter. Jessica felt angry tears threatening to spill down her cheeks. She couldn't stand one more second of everyone accusing her and reveling in her humiliation. She bolted from the Moon Beach Café, wanting to get as far away as possible from the prying eyes of Sweet Valley.

"Jess!" Elizabeth called behind her.

Outside, Jessica jumped into the twins' red Jeep. All she wanted was to get home and hide under the covers for the rest of her life.

Elizabeth approached the driver's side of the Jeep, her face concerned. "You okay?" she asked Jessica softly.

Hearing the gentle worry in her sister's voice, Jessica couldn't hold back her tears any longer. "Nobody believes me, Liz," she sobbed.

"I know," Elizabeth said simply. Unfortunately, there was no bright side to what had happened at the art show.

"I didn't pose naked," Jessica said, willing her twin to believe her. "I'd never do that."

"What do you expect, Jess, after what you told Enid?" Elizabeth asked.

"Nothing happened. He painted me, that's all. He wouldn't even let me see the picture."

When Elizabeth didn't say anything, Jessica felt a fresh wave of tears coming on. "Not you too!" She was silent for a moment. "I didn't do it, Liz. You've got to believe me." If Elizabeth didn't believe her, no one would.

"Why should I?" Elizabeth asked.

"Because I'm your sister. And I need you." Tears ran down Jessica's cheeks, and she felt as if her heart would break.

Elizabeth leaned into the Jeep and hugged her sister tightly. "What can I do?" she whispered.

"Help me get rid of the painting," Jessica answered. She breathed deeply, willing herself to regain control of her emotions. Having Elizabeth on her side made her feel strong enough to face the situation. It was time to take action.

"Jessica, you can't," Elizabeth said. At the look her sister gave her, she added, "Do you think I like this? There are fifty creeps on the answering machine asking for dates."

"For me?" Jessica asked. Usually she would love to hear that fifty guys wanted dates—but these were *not* usual circumstances.

"For either one of us. It's humiliating." Elizabeth paused. Since Jessica and Elizabeth looked exactly alike, a nude painting of one of them was as bad as a nude painting of the other. "I'm in that painting, too," Elizabeth continued.

"But stealing it isn't going to change what everybody believes."

"Then how?" Jessica asked. She wasn't about to let people all over the United States see her naked.

Elizabeth finally smiled. "I've been your sister too long not to have learned a thing or two," she said, a mischievous twinkle in her eye.

Elizabeth walked into the art room where Dakota Dancer was working on a new painting. She crossed the room, ready to confront him.

She gestured at Dakota's canvas. "Is she going to be nude, too?" she asked sarcastically.

"I'm working," Dakota answered. He sounded annoyed, and he showed no interest in speaking to Elizabeth.

"Oh, that's right. The great artist needs silence while he dreams up new ways to exploit teenage girls." Elizabeth stared at him, wondering how he would respond. Just the sight of him made her feel like punching someone.

"Art is freedom. I paint what I feel." Dakota's tone was self-righteous and indifferent. Obviously he wasn't intimidated by Elizabeth Wakefield.

"And you felt my sister was naked, even though she was wearing a bathing suit." Elizabeth's voice was filled with contempt.

"I captured the spirit and beauty of the

human form. Clothes are immaterial." Dakota glanced at her, then went back to his painting.

"So she was never nude?" Elizabeth asked.

"No. She didn't need to be."

"Don't you care what this is doing to her reputation?" Elizabeth asked vehemently. "How would you feel—"

"I'm an artist, not a model," Dakota interrupted. He seemed to consider the subject closed.

A couple of hours later, the whole gang was gathered in the Wakefields' kitchen. They were crowded around the modern-looking kitchen island, and their eyes were glued to the small tape recorder that Elizabeth had placed on the counter. She'd recorded her whole conversation with Dakota Dancer, and now everyone was listening intently as she played it back.

"No. She didn't need to be," Dakota's voice said over the tape.

"Don't you care what this is doing to her reputation? How would you feel—" Everyone was silent as Elizabeth's voice came out loud and clear in the quiet kitchen.

"I'm an artist, not a model," they heard Dakota answer.

Elizabeth switched off the tape and looked at the surprised faces around her. Jessica was actually smiling for the first time since Dakota's painting had been unveiled.

"Dakota. What a jerk," Winston said. He pounded his fist on the counter.

"That could've been me," Enid said, gulping.

"I'm gonna kill that guy," Todd growled.

"I am so embarrassed," Lila said, gesturing wildly. "I think Jessica is owed a major apology here." Everyone stared at Lila, who was tapping her foot impatiently on the kitchen floor.

"Well, I'm waiting," she said.

"What about you?" Patty asked. They all remembered that Lila had been the first to accuse Jessica of having posed nude.

"I never had any doubts," Lila said, her voice innocent. "After all, Jessica is my best friend." In a hot-pink blouse and black miniskirt, Lila was as chic as always—but she did look a bit uncomfortable.

Winston reached behind him and grabbed a large manila envelope. "I guess these belong to you," he said, handing the envelope of photographs to Jessica. He sounded contrite, and he was smiling shyly.

"Thank you," Jessica said, clutching the envelope.

"You have no idea how much that hurt," Winston told her, running a hand through his messy dark hair.

Jessica arched her eyebrows. "Negatives," she demanded, holding out her hand.

Reluctantly Winston brought a strip of negatives out from under the counter. Jessica reached for them, but she had to tug with all her might to get them out of Winston's grip. When she finally got them in her hands, Winston smiled sheepishly.

"Elizabeth, you were great. Thanks a lot," Jessica said.

"Hey, I'm your sister," Elizabeth responded. "But we still have one big problem. The painting."

Jessica shrugged, and she had a characteristic glimmer in her eye. "Oh, I think I've got a way to handle that."

Jessica glided into the Los Angeles art gallery where Dakota's work was going to be shown. The official opening was the next night, and Dakota was putting the finishing touches on the installation.

"Hi, Dakota," Jessica said sweetly. She sauntered up to his side, smiling, and glanced around the posh gallery. "Wow, everything looks great. This is so cool. I can't wait until the opening tomorrow night."

Dakota finished what he was doing and looked at Jessica. "Your sister doesn't feel that way," he remarked.

"Oh, her," Jessica said, waving a hand dismissively. "She doesn't understand art. I swear, if we weren't identical, I wouldn't even believe we were related." Jessica could tell that Dakota believed every word she said.

She took advantage of Dakota's massive ego and went in for the kill. "Don't you think it's time we celebrate?" she asked. "You, me, the beach. Let's go back to where you made it all happen."

When Dakota smiled and nodded, Jessica knew she had him exactly where she wanted him. She gave herself a mental pat on the back, wondering how she could ever have thought that Dakota Dancer would get the best of her.

An hour later, Jessica and Dakota were lounging on a blanket next to the lake. They'd eaten a picnic dinner, and now Jessica was ready to put the final steps of her plan in motion.

"Wow, it's really hot out here," she said, her voice sultry. "Let's go for a swim."

Jessica stood up and reached for Dakota's hand. He protested as she pulled him up. "I didn't bring my suit."

"Who needs them?" Jessica said, shrugging. "We have nothing to hide from each other."

"Okay." Dakota began to undo the straps of his denim overalls.

"Oh, I forgot my towel in the car. I'll meet you out there," Jessica said. Dakota nodded and continued to undress.

Jessica ran to the Jeep and signaled to her friends, who were waiting a small distance away. The group ran toward the lake, trying not to laugh.

"Oh, Dakota?" Jessica called.

When Dakota turned around, he was completely naked. Winston snapped a few quick pictures, and everyone whistled.

"What are you doing?" yelled Dakota, attempting to cover himself with the boots and clothes he'd thrown on the ground.

"Some local *wild*life photography," Lila called.

"Just capturing the beauty of the human form," Elizabeth said, smiling at him.

"How do you like it, Dakota?" Jessica asked. She was loving every second of her revenge.

"Give me that camera," Dakota shouted angrily.

Winston threw the camera to Patty, who waved it in front of her. "Can't do it," Patty said, smirking. She tossed the camera to Enid.

Enid caught the camera easily. "Hot potato," she called, handing it to Todd.

"Don't even think about it," Todd said, staring at Dakota through his dark sunglasses.

Jessica decided that it was time to get down to business. "Okay, Dakota, here's the deal. You either cut my portrait from the show or the whole school gets to see you without your . . . boots."

"Forget it," he answered uneasily.

"It's your call," Elizabeth said. She threw her arm around her sister and laughed out loud.

The next afternoon, everyone had flocked to the art gallery for Dakota's opening. As they'd expected,

Dakota had changed the painting so that Jessica was wearing her leopard-print bikini.

"Wow, Jess, it's really beautiful," Todd said, admiring the painting. Even if Dakota was a scummy person, he *was* a talented artist.

"Personally, I prefer the original," Winston said. Then he ducked as Todd took a playful punch at him. "Not that this isn't nice, too."

"Excuse me, I have something to take care of," Jessica said, spotting Dakota on the other side of the room.

Meanwhile, Elizabeth had caught sight of Mr. Cooper. She approached him, hoping that this conversation would be friendlier than their last one.

"Mr. Cooper, I want to apologize for what I said to you. I'm going to print a retraction in tomorrow's *Oracle*," Elizabeth said sincerely.

Ever since this whole thing with Jessica had blown up, she'd realized that public exposure could really hurt someone's feelings. Before, she hadn't considered how Mr. Cooper must have perceived the constant attack on him and his bald head.

"Elizabeth, as painful as it may be for me to accept, *you* were right," Mr. Cooper responded.

"I don't get it." Elizabeth couldn't believe that the principal was backing down. This was the last thing she'd expected.

"We all have to use judgment in matters of

censorship. In my case, I overreacted." Mr. Cooper seemed contrite, and he was smiling kindly.

"Do you really mean that?" Elizabeth asked, still slightly confused.

"Check out the graffiti wall tomorrow. You'll find my picture back up there." Apparently Jessica's disastrous experience had made him realize that a comical picture of his head wasn't such a big deal.

Elizabeth grinned at Sweet Valley High's enlightened principal, then crossed the room to where Jessica was confronting Dakota.

"I believe you have something for me," Dakota said. He held out his hand.

"I guess I won't be needing these," Jessica said, handing him a roll of exposed film.

Dakota grabbed the film. Without a backward glance, he stalked off across the room.

"How do you know he won't change it back?" Elizabeth asked, taking a few steps toward her twin.

Jessica pulled a second roll of film out of the pocket of her bright red jacket and held it up. "Call it insurance," she said with a confident gleam in her eye.

CRITICAL MESS

Based on the teleplay by
Sheldon Krasner & David Saling

On a sunny afternoon, Bruce Patman and Manuel Lopez sat in a booth at the Moon Beach Café, sharing a huge plate of french fries.

"Why don't we take in the volleyball tournament Sunday?" Manny asked Bruce. "We're talking *babe* fest."

Bruce shook his head. "I can't. I've got to pick up my uncle Andy at the airport."

"Tell him to take a cab," Manuel answered.

"He's a big-time director of commercials," Bruce said. "He's used to limos. I can't tell him to take a cab." It was no surprise to Manny that a member of Bruce's family would be rich, successful, and accustomed to elegance.

Elizabeth Wakefield was sitting in the booth behind Bruce and Manuel, and she couldn't help overhearing what Bruce had said about his uncle. When her boyfriend, Todd Wilkins, slid into the booth, she leaned forward.

"Guess what? Bruce's uncle, a big-time director, is coming to Sweet Valley. Maybe he's making a movie here." She'd been practically bursting with the news.

"Unreal," Todd answered. He'd just come from basketball practice, and now set the ball down on the seat of the booth. "I'll be right back," he said, already halfway across the diner on a search for some ketchup.

"Hey, Todd, you got a quarter?" Winston Egbert called. "I'm on my last toad warrior." Winston had been playing one of the Moon Beach Café's video games.

"Sure," Todd said, handing him a coin. "You know, Liz just heard Bruce's uncle may be shooting a big action movie in town."

Winston's eyes lit up. "No way. I wonder if he's doing that new one with Keanu Reeves and Brad Pitt."

"Awesome," Patty Gilbert whispered to herself. She'd been sitting at the counter of the Moon Beach, listening to the conversation between Winston and Todd. She sprang from her stool when she saw Enid Rollins standing nearby.

"Enid, you'll never believe it," Patty said, overcome with excitement. "Bruce Patman's uncle is making a new movie here starring Brad Pitt and Christian Slater!"

Enid looked as if she were going to faint.

"Omigod. Christian Slater? I love him!" She began jumping up and down, barely able to contain herself.

"Me too. I've just gotta meet them," Patty said. Her big brown eyes were sparkling.

"How?" Enid asked.

"They'll need extras," Patty pointed out.

"You mean they're casting here? Omigod."

Enid raced over to the corner booth where Lila Fowler and Jessica Wakefield were sitting. "Guys, check this out," Enid shouted. "Christian Slater, Ethan Hawke, and Enid Rollins starring in a new film directed by Bruce Patman's uncle. What do you think?"

Jessica gave Enid one of her most condescending glances. "I think your pantyhose are too tight," she said.

"I'm telling you, it's true," Enid insisted. "He's here casting his next big movie." She sighed dramatically. "If I'm gonna be discovered, I've gotta go buy a new . . . everything! See ya."

"That's ridiculous," Jessica said once Enid had rushed off.

"Of course it is," Lila agreed.

"Why would Bruce Patman's uncle be casting in Sweet Valley?" Jessica asked as the girls exchanged a meaningful glance.

"Completely absurd."

"So, are we shopping?" Jessica said.

Lila nodded vigorously, her black beret

bouncing on her head. "House of Chic. After rehearsal."

Lila and Jessica were both in Sweet Valley High's next school play, *Macbeth*. They had to rehearse every day after school, but they still had plenty of free time to shop. And House of Chic was one of the best stores in Sweet Valley.

Lila and Jessica stood up, leaving several dollar bills on the table. They walked halfway out the door of the Moon Beach Café, then turned around abruptly. They'd both noticed Bruce sitting in a booth with Manny.

Lila reached Bruce's side first. She sat down next to him and put a hand on his shoulder. "Bruce, you've got to introduce me to your uncle!"

"Lila!" Jessica said. She'd taken the seat next to Manny, but she was leaning across the table so that her face was just inches from Bruce's. "Bruce, I'm sure you're aware I'm starring as Lady Macbeth this weekend in the school play."

"Really?" Bruce made a face at Manny, apparently enjoying the fact that Lila and Jessica were suddenly kissing up to him.

"I'm in it, too. I have a pivotal role," Lila said.

"Oh, sure, Witch Number Two," Jessica scoffed. She wasn't about to let Lila steal her spotlight.

"Typecasting?" Bruce asked sarcastically.

"Why don't I leave two tickets at the door for

you and a guest?" Jessica went on. She wanted to give Lila as little chance as possible to say anything.

"I'll go," Manny said.

Jessica glared at Manny. "An out-of-town guest," she said pointedly.

"Better yet, I'll reserve you a whole row. Whatever your uncle needs," Lila said. She put both her arms around Bruce so that he was forced to look at her.

"I'll go," Manny repeated.

"Whoa, retract your claws," Bruce said as he disentangled himself from Lila. "Uncle Andy won't be here until after the play closes. Save your tickets for someone with time to waste."

"I'll go," Manny said for the third time. Both Jessica and Lila ignored him, getting up to leave. "So where do I pick up the tickets?" Manny asked.

Making a face, Jessica finally turned to look at Manny. "At the door—seven-fifty apiece."

"Hey, Steven," Jessica said. She'd been searching all morning for Steven, who was scheduled to review *Macbeth*.

"Hi, Jessica. How about an interview for the *Oracle?* I'm reviewing your play." He smiled amiably.

"No, you're not," Jessica said. "I mean, not

when you've got two tickets to a Pearl Jam concert," she added quickly.

"I wish."

"Wishes can come true." She pulled two tickets out of her bag. She'd had to cash in a lot of favors to get them, but she knew her efforts would be worth it when she got the lead in Andy Patman's latest blockbuster film.

"Since I'm starring in *Macbeth*, I can't use them," she explained, trying to sound disappointed.

"It's a nice offer, but . . ." Steven's voice trailed off, and Jessica could tell that he was dying to take the tickets.

"Which would you rather review, a four-hundred-year-old play or the hottest group in the world?" Jessica asked. By the look in Steven's eyes, she knew exactly what his answer was going to be. "The paper can get someone to fill in for you."

When Steven took the tickets, Jessica breathed a deep sigh of relief. She was on her way to fame and fortune.

Mr. Collins walked up to Elizabeth, who was bent over one of the *Oracle*'s computers, working on her latest piece for the school newspaper.

"Liz, I need you to review the school play," he said.

"What happened to Steven?" she asked.

"He suddenly came into some Pearl Jam tickets. He's going to cover the concert for us." Mr. Collins shrugged.

"Are you sure you want me to review *Macbeth?*" Elizabeth had no desire to review her own sister—she hated to think about Jessica's reaction if Elizabeth didn't hail her as the next Sharon Stone or Winona Ryder.

"Why, do you have a problem with the classics?" Mr. Collins asked.

"Not the classics, my sister. She's starring in it." Even as she explained the situation to Mr. Collins, Elizabeth had a feeling she was stuck. The *Oracle* advisor could be pretty hard to budge once he made up his mind about something.

"You're the one we always rely on in a pinch," Mr. Collins responded easily. "I know you can be objective."

Elizabeth sighed. Mr. Collins didn't have to live with Jessica—the girl who probably didn't even know the word *objective* was in the dictionary.

Winston, Patty, Lila, and Jessica were sitting at a table in Sweet Valley High's outdoor courtyard, finishing their lunches.

Winston turned to Jessica, a hopeful grin on his face. "You know, Jess, I've been thinking. Seeing as I'm playing Macbeth and you're Lady

106

Macbeth and they're married, maybe you and I should . . . you know, do some of the things that married people do."

Jessica stood up, glancing contemptuously at Winston. His attempts to get a date with her had started to border on the pathetic.

"Great idea, Winston," she said in a mock cheerful voice. "You can start by straightening up my locker, then pick up the latest issue of *Sassy*, and on the way home you can drop off my cheer-leading outfit at the cleaners." She started to walk away, but Winston stopped her. His eyes were practically popping out of his head.

"And then?" he asked.

"Take a cold shower."

"Ouch." Winston didn't press the matter any further.

Enid rushed over to the table, as full of energy as usual. "Hey, everybody, we're a hit. I just came from the box office, and we're sold out."

"Duh," Jessica said, rolling her eyes. "I'm the lead. What did you expect?"

"Too bad Bruce's uncle won't be there," Patty said sadly. "He might have discovered one of us."

"He still will, after reading my great review," Jessica commented.

Now that she'd organized things so that Elizabeth was covering the play for the school newspaper, she knew she'd get a rave review. First of all, she knew her performance would be nothing short of brilliant. And second, who could pan their own twin sister?

"Aren't you being a bit optimistic?" Lila asked. "We don't open until tomorrow."

"Just a formality," Jessica said confidently. "Liz is reviewing the play."

An hour later Jessica walked into the *Oracle* office. She put on her nicest face, then strolled over to the paper's student technician. He looked absorbed in the task of replacing the printer's toner cartridge, but Jessica figured she wouldn't have much trouble getting his attention.

"Oh, Chucky," she said, her voice low and sultry.

"What did I do?" he asked. Like most guys, he was fairly nervous around Jessica.

"Relax, Chuck. I just felt we should get to know each other better." She stepped a little closer, and she could see Chuck's interest in her written all over his face.

"We should?" he asked, sounding surprised.

Jessica nodded. "And what better way to get to know someone than by doing them a favor?"

"You want to do me a favor?" he asked, sounding even more surprised.

Jessica laughed. "That's very funny, Chuck. No. I want *you* to do *me* a favor." She reached into her backpack and dug out an envelope. Then she handed Chuck an eight-by-ten glossy photograph of herself. In the picture, she was wearing a bikini that showed off every curve of her body. "Do you see this picture?" she asked.

Chuck gulped. "Oh, good God, yes."

"I want you to deliver this photo along with a copy of the theater review the second it comes off the presses." She paused for a moment, allowing Chuck to appreciate the photograph. "It goes to Andy Patman, a guest at Sweet Valley Lodge. Think you could do that for me?"

"We can't give out copies until—"

"Do this for me and there's an autographed photo in it for you," Jessica said quickly.

Chuck nodded, and Jessica just hoped that he wouldn't drool all over her picture. She wanted the photo to be in perfect condition when it reached the hands of Andy Patman—the man who was going to make her a star.

Todd and Elizabeth found their seats in Sweet Valley High's auditorium just before *Macbeth* was about to begin. Elizabeth loved the theater, but she still had some misgivings about having to review her own sister.

"I can't believe you wanted to come," she said to Todd as he settled into the seat beside her. Usually Todd didn't like live performances unless they involved a bunch of sweaty guys and some kind of ball.

"Me either," he agreed. "But I've got a paper

due on *Macbeth*, and now I don't have to read the Cliffs Notes."

Todd and Elizabeth grew quiet as the lights dimmed. For better or worse, the play had begun.

Onstage, Winston stared at a dagger that was hanging from an almost invisible thread in front of him. "Is this a dagger which I see before me, the handle toward my hand?" he said, his voice booming through the auditorium. "Come let me clutch thee."

Winston reached for the dagger. Unfortunately, his hand gripped the knife blade, rather than the handle, and a look of pain immediately crossed his face.

"Ow!" he yelped. Then, remembering he was onstage, he hastily corrected himself. "Oweth! That hurteth. Blood runneth from my hand. O would that I had some gauze." Winston had broken out of character, but his performance was still entertaining. And he *had* managed some pretty convincing ad lib lines. Elizabeth was impressed.

Jessica entered the stage from the wings. She looked beautiful in a regal gown with her hair piled on top of her head. "Ew. Yuck!" she screeched when she saw Winston's hand dripping with real blood.

Winston was valiantly trying to go on with the show, and now he turned somberly to Jessica. He gestured for her to continue with her lines, but she remained silent. She was just staring at Winston's hand, a disgusted look on her face.

"Lady Macbeth, thou hast cast a heavy shadow across my face. Thou upstageth me for thine own gain," Winston improvised.

Jessica wailed mournfully, then walked offstage. When she reappeared later, she seemed to have composed herself after Winston's disaster with the knife.

"Out, damned spot! Out, I say! Why, then 'tis time to do't. Hell is murky," Jessica recited. It wasn't clear to Elizabeth that Jessica had any idea what the words she was saying actually *meant*. "Fie, my lord, fie!" she continued.

Suddenly Jessica's eyes fell on someone in the audience. Her cute-guy radar went on immediately, and she couldn't help flirting. "Hi, my lord, hi," she said to the guy in the front row.

Then Jessica became aware that she was acting in a tragic play and got back into her character of Lady Macbeth. "A solder and afeard? What need we fear . . ."

In her seat, Elizabeth frowned to herself. She already had a bad feeling about the review she was going to have to write for the newspaper.

Later in the play Enid, Patty, and Lila stood around a papier-mâché cauldron. They were dressed in extravagant witch costumes, and they were tossing fake ingredients into the cauldron.

"For a charm of pow'rful trouble, like a hell-broth boil and bubble," Lila shouted.

Jessica wandered out from the wings and across the stage behind Patty, Enid, and Lila. She was moaning and groaning, pretending that she was about to swoon.

The girls playing the witches stopped and stared at Jessica. She wasn't supposed to be on-stage during their scene. Apparently she'd taken it upon herself to reinvent the role of Lady Macbeth.

"Wow, Jess has a huge part," Todd whispered to Elizabeth. "She's in every scene."

Elizabeth grimaced. "That would be news to Shakespeare," she whispered back.

"Huh?" Todd asked.

"Put it this way: You'd better read the book."

Finally Jessica drifted offstage again. As she left, Patty, Enid, and Lila glared in her direction. Then they threw more ingredients into their cauldron.

"Double, double, toil and trouble; fire burn and cauldron bubble," they chanted aloud.

Watching the group onstage, Elizabeth had a feeling they were trying to put a curse on Jessica.

Monday morning, the cast members of *Macbeth* waited impatiently next to an empty

Oracle paper rack. They were all anxious to read Elizabeth's review.

"I wonder what Liz is gonna say about the play," Patty said.

"Let's see," Jessica said, gesturing with her hands as if she were turning the pages of an imaginary paper. "'A brilliant performance. A stunning interpretation. A tour de force. Two thumbs up.'"

"I didn't think we were that good," Enid said.

"We? I was talking about me."

Jessica was never modest, but she didn't need to be. She knew she was probably the most gifted person in all of Sweet Valley—or in all of California, for that matter.

"As always, Jessica, you're your own biggest fan," Lila said.

The group was interrupted by Chuck, who appeared with a fresh stack of newspapers. After he loaded the papers into the rack, all of the cast members descended upon them.

Patty was the first to locate the review. "Here it is, page eight."

"'Winston Egbert gave a beautifully anguished performance as Macbeth. His pain seemed real,'" Winston read aloud. He was beaming, and his face was flushed with pride. He held up his bandaged hand for everyone to see. "She got that right," he added.

"'The witches, played by Patty Gilbert,

Enid Rollins, and Lila Fowler, had a hauntingly delightful presence,'" Enid read from her copy of the paper.

Lila cleared her throat. "'Ms. Fowler lent an especially professional tone to the production.' *Très* excellent."

Jessica's eyes searched through the review. She was bored with hearing about everyone else's performance. "Where am I? Elizabeth must be saving the best for last."

Everyone's eyes turned to Jessica as Lila started to read the end of the review. "'And the role of Lady Macbeth was overperformed and loosely interpreted by Jessica Wakefield.'"

A heavy silence fell upon the group, and everyone stared at Jessica.

"Overperformed and loosely interpreted!" Jessica shrieked. "She trashed me. My film career is ruined."

Jessica leaned back against a locker, crushed. She couldn't believe that Elizabeth had stabbed her in the back. She would never forgive her.

Jessica stormed into the *Oracle* office. She had about a million things she wanted to say to Elizabeth—and none of them was very sisterly.

"Okay, where is she?" Jessica said to the roomful of people who were working in the office.

When everyone turned and gaped at her, she felt even angrier. "What are you all looking at?" she snapped.

"Oh, hi, Jess. I didn't see you come in," Elizabeth said calmly.

"How could you do this to me?" Jessica wailed. "You're my sister. You could have at least been kind."

Elizabeth raised her eyebrows. "Believe me, I was."

"That's low. No, it's worse than that." Jessica had never been so mad in her life. "Now we know who the evil twin is."

Jessica headed out of the office, but she was stopped by Chuck. He held out a copy of the photograph she'd given him.

"You forgot to autograph it," he said.

Jessica grabbed the picture and tore it viciously into several pieces. Without another word, she stomped out of the office.

"Hmmm, wallet size," Chuck said, studying what was left of the picture.

After school, Jessica sat in a booth at the Moon Beach Café. She didn't even feel like eating a Mega-burger—a sure sign that she was truly depressed.

"Come on, Jess, cheer up," Patty said.

"It's just the school paper," Enid added. "It's not that important."

"But it certainly is absorbent," Winston said. He was mopping up some of his spilled soda with his copy of the *Oracle*.

"What effect could a school-paper review have?" Patty wondered aloud.

As Jessica continued to frown at her food, Lila came into the Moon Beach as if she were walking on air.

"Guess which Sweet Valley socialite is going to be featured in Andy Patman's newest production?" she said with a flourish.

There was no doubt in anyone's mind that Lila was referring to herself.

"With Christian Slater?" Enid asked.

"What about Brad Pitt?" Patty said.

"Let's just say it's a delicious cast," Lila answered, sliding into the booth.

Everyone began to congratulate Lila, but Jessica just glared at her. "How did you get the job?" she asked. Lila's getting *her* role made her feel even worse.

"I ran into Andy at his hotel," Lila said casually.

"What were you doing there?" Jessica asked suspiciously.

"Dropping off Liz's review." Lila smiled serenely at her best friend.

"I can't believe you would do something like that," Jessica huffed. "That is *so* tacky."

Lila smirked. "I see. Well, how might that

compare with your sending over the review *and* a picture of yourself in a bikini? Would you consider what I did to be more tacky, less tacky, or about the same?"

Jessica felt like spitting in Lila's face, but she didn't say anything. She didn't have a chance.

"Well, gotta go report for my wardrobe fitting," Lila gloated. "*Ciao.*"

Lila waved at the group, then sashayed out of the Moon Beach. Her eyes narrowed, Jessica watched her friend leave. Lila thought she'd won, but Jessica knew better. She was going to get into the movie. No matter what.

Elizabeth watched Jessica take a bottle of diet soda from the Wakefields' large refrigerator. Jessica hadn't spoken to her since the terrible scene in the *Oracle* office, and it was driving Elizabeth crazy.

"Come on, Jess. You can't be mad at me forever," Elizabeth said. When Jessica didn't respond, Elizabeth tried another tactic. "I didn't ask for the job. It was assigned to me."

Jessica slammed the door of the refrigerator and headed for the family room. Elizabeth put down the empty glass she was holding and followed her twin. She could be as stubborn as her sister, and right now she was determined to make up with Jessica.

"I didn't mean to hurt you," Elizabeth said softly, sitting down next to Jessica on the sofa. "I had to be objective."

Jessica remained stonily silent, and Elizabeth was beginning to feel desperate. "This is ridiculous. You're blowing it way out of proportion," she said.

Again Jessica said nothing. For the first time Elizabeth really understood the expression "like talking to a brick wall." She cleared her throat and tried one more time. "Will you please say something?" she begged.

"Go away," Jessica answered.

"That's something." Elizabeth felt slightly—very slightly—relieved.

"You didn't want me to star in that movie and become famous. You're jealous, so you're trying to hold me back," Jessica shouted.

"Hold you back?" Elizabeth couldn't believe that Jessica actually thought she was jealous.

"I wanted that part more than anything I've ever wanted in my life, and your stupid review cost me the job."

"How?" Elizabeth asked. As far as she could tell, Jessica wasn't making any sense.

"Andy Patman read it, okay?" Jessica said, sounding genuinely upset. "And based on that, Lila's in the movie and I'm not. I'll never get to be a star, thanks to you."

Jessica fled upstairs to her room. Elizabeth sat

alone on the family room couch, feeling like the world's worst sister. She had to help Jessica get a part in Andy Patman's movie.

But how?

Elizabeth and Todd pulled up to a film studio just outside of Sweet Valley. She'd called Bruce and begged him to tell her where his uncle was working. She'd insisted the situation was an emergency, and in her mind it really was.

"I hope this works," Elizabeth said as she turned off the ignition. "Jessica is hardly talking to me."

"And you're complaining?" Todd asked. He would have considered that kind of situation a blessing.

When they got out of the car, Elizabeth saw a sign on the studio's heavy steel door. "Closed set. Looks like we can't go in."

Now that Todd was here, he wanted to check out the filming of a big Hollywood movie. "Come on. What are they gonna do to us?"

As they stood deliberating whether or not to go inside, a man tried to push past them.

"You coming or going?" he asked impatiently.

"Coming," Todd said.

"Going," Elizabeth said at the same time. She was used to following rules.

"Well, either way, you're blocking the door." Again the man tried to get past them.

"Do you know where we could find Mr. Patman?" Todd asked politely.

"You'll find me inside, if you let me through." He reached around Elizabeth and opened the door. Todd and Elizabeth exchanged surprised glances.

"Well, I guess if Andy Patman himself says we can go in . . ." Elizabeth said.

"Let's go!" Todd finished for her.

Elizabeth and Todd followed him inside, taking in the sound stage and all of the people who were running around frantically. There were wires and lights all over the place.

"Tell the cameraman I want to open with a low shot from here," Andy Patman said.

Elizabeth steeled her nerves as she walked up to Bruce's uncle. She'd never spoken to a famous director before. "Uh, excuse me, Mr. Patman. Can I talk with you for a minute?"

He glanced at her, then looked back at the camera crew. "Can you make it brief? I'm running behind."

Elizabeth nodded. "I'm Elizabeth Wakefield, and this is my boyfriend, Todd. I reviewed *Macbeth* for my school paper, the *Oracle*." Elizabeth was speaking as fast as she could, but Todd nudged her in the ribs.

"He said *brief*," Todd whispered.

"Right. I understand you saw a copy of it and hired my friend Lila Fowler because of my review, and—"

"You think that's why I hired her?" Mr. Patman interjected. "Look, I needed somebody about Lila's height and size, and she showed up on my doorstep. It's that simple."

Elizabeth didn't know what to say.

"You mean her review didn't have anything to do with your decision?" Todd asked.

"Hardly." Mr. Patman laughed.

"Looks like you're off the hook, Liz," Todd said.

"Say, have you ever done any acting?" Mr. Patman asked Elizabeth. He was looking at her as if she were a lab specimen.

"M-me? Why?" Elizabeth stammered.

"Somebody just dropped out, and I think you'd be perfect for the part. You're a very pretty girl."

"Thanks, but acting really isn't my thing," Elizabeth said graciously. Then a light bulb went on in her head. "On the other hand, my twin sister is fantastic."

"Great. We shoot the commercial at nine tomorrow morning." The director walked away, leaving Todd and Elizabeth staring at his retreating back.

"Did he say commercial?" Todd asked.

They looked at each other and burst out laughing. Elizabeth had a feeling that Brad Pitt and Christian Slater weren't going to be part of the ensemble cast after all.

*　　*　　*

Lila and Manny stood at the counter of the Moon Beach Café, and Manny was grilling Lila about her upcoming role in Andy Patman's movie.

"So, how big a part do you have?" Manuel asked.

"The overall message of the piece depends on it," Lila responded. She was bending the truth a little, but creative lying was one of her greatest skills.

"Well, I hope you still remember me when you're famous," Manny joked.

"I'm sorry—your name is . . . ?" Lila teased back, using a snobby Hollywood voice.

Jessica winced as she listened to Lila and Manny laughing. She and Patty were eavesdropping on Lila from a nearby booth.

"She is being so gross," Patty said to Jessica. "I can't believe she got that part and you didn't. You must be sick with envy."

Jessica smiled serenely as her gaze fell on a WET FLOOR sign that was standing next to their booth. "No, Patty. That was the old me. I've discovered that life is too short. I'm above all that now."

Out of the corner of her eye, Jessica saw Lila stand up and slip on her jacket. "Well, Hollywood awaits," Lila said loudly enough for Patty and Jessica to overhear her.

"I know you'll be great, Lila," Manny called after her. "Break a leg!"

When Lila turned and waved at Manuel, Jessica discreetly slid the WET FLOOR sign under the table of the booth. Then she waited, with her fingers crossed, for Lila to walk by.

Just as Lila started to pass Jessica she skidded on the slippery floor. Her left foot flew out from under her, and almost in slow motion, Lila crashed to the floor. "Aaahh!" she screamed at the top of her lungs.

All eyes in the Moon Beach turned to Lila, who was lying on the floor, gripping her ankle and sobbing. Jessica tried not to smile as she pushed the WET FLOOR sign out into the open again.

"Why me?" Lila moaned.

Jessica got up from the booth and gave Lila what she hoped looked like a sympathetic pat on the back. Then Jessica walked toward the exit of the Moon Beach Café, ready to proceed with her plan.

"Why me?" Lila was still moaning. "Why me?"

Jessica giggled to herself as she stepped out into the bright sun of the parking lot. Just then Elizabeth and Todd pulled up, honking the horn as they got close to her.

"Jess, I'm glad I found you," Elizabeth called.

Jessica continued across the lot, refusing to acknowledge her sister. Even though she'd fixed the situation with Lila, she was still worried about whether or not she was going to get the part. And she wasn't about to forgive her twin—Elizabeth needed to suffer for a couple more days, at least.

"I think you oughta listen to this," Todd said to Jessica. His voice was so authoritative that she wanted to scream.

"What?" she asked indignantly.

Elizabeth grinned, and her blue-green eyes were sparkling. "I convinced Andy Patman to give you a part," she exclaimed.

"If this is some kind of joke . . . ," Jessica said slowly.

Elizabeth shook her head, and Jessica felt her heart pound with excitement. Things were turning out even better than she'd hoped.

"That's fantastic!" Jessica shouted, reaching out to hug her sister. "In that case, I forgive you."

Elizabeth glanced at Todd, wondering how she should break the news that Andy Patman wasn't making a feature-length film. "I don't know if it's as good a part as Lila's, but—"

"Whatever," Jessica said, shrugging. Of course, Elizabeth didn't yet know that Lila was out of commission. Jessica jumped into the Jeep and buckled her seat belt.

"But I haven't finished telling you—" Elizabeth started to say.

"Whatever," Jessica repeated, turning the key

in the Jeep's ignition. She shut the door and gunned the engine.

"The only thing is, it's not a movie. It's a—"

"Whatever," Jessica mouthed through the closed window of the Jeep. She peeled out of the parking lot, music blaring.

With a wry look at each other, Elizabeth and Todd turned to the door of the Moon Beach Café just as Patty walked out. She was propping up Lila, who was limping beside her.

Lila was shouting into a cellular phone. "And get me Dr. Waldman! I don't care if he's in surgery! Do you know who I am?"

She continued to limp toward her car, pulling Patty behind her. Elizabeth watched Lila hobble along, wondering if Jessica had had anything to do with Lila's new injury. Somehow Elizabeth had a feeling that the answer to that question was yes.

At nine o'clock in the morning, the whole Sweet Valley gang had gathered in the studio where Andy Patman was filming. There was a lavishly outfitted kitchen set, and people were running in every direction. By this point, the fact that Mr. Patman was filming a commercial—not a movie—had become fairly clear. At least, Brad Pitt and Christian Slater were nowhere to be found.

"Well, Bruce, I've got to get this shoot going,"

Mr. Patman said. "You and your friends will be fine right here." He pointed to some folding chairs that had been set up in front of the set, and everyone scrambled to get seats.

"Thanks, Uncle Andy," Bruce responded.

"Wow, this is cool," Winston said to Bruce. "That kitchen set looks so real! Do you think the sink really works?"

"Of course not. They're just props. None of them actually works," Bruce said, his tone patronizing.

"Yeah, Eggplant, don't you know anything about show business?" Manny added.

Over on the set, one of the cameramen walked over to the sink in the kitchen. He took a glass from a cabinet and turned on the tap water. Then he filled up his glass and took a few gulps.

Winston laughed. "I suppose that's *prop* water. Some sort of special effect, maybe?" he teased Bruce and Manny.

Several yards away, Jessica was having her hair brushed by the stylist on the set. She couldn't wait to get in front of the camera, especially because Lila was out of the picture. Now Jessica knew she'd be the star without having to share the spotlight with her pushy best friend.

Patty stood next to Jessica, nodding her approval of the way the stylist was arranging Jessica's hair. "Wow, that was really nice of Liz

126

to talk to Bruce's uncle for you," she said.

"Yeah, yeah, she's a saint," Jessica said, cutting off that line of conversation. "Anyway, now that Lila's had an unfortunate accident, I've got the inside track on her part."

"Don't count on it," Patty said, nodding toward the door. Lila had just barged into the studio.

Jessica's mouth dropped open. "She showed up? All right, two can play that game. Excuse me a moment."

Jessica pulled away from the stylist, who was still fixing her hair, and headed over to where Lila was standing.

"Hi, Mr. Patman. Sorry I'm late," Lila said. She was leaning on a pair of crutches, but she appeared calm and looked as fashionable as always.

"What happened to you?" Mr. Patman asked. He'd been studying some notes on a clipboard, but now he stared at Lila.

"Oh, it's nothing really," she said casually. "I just twisted my ankle slightly. Minor sprain." She tried to take a step without using her crutches. "Ow."

Mr. Patman shook his head and ran his fingers through his hair. He looked tired, irritated, and worried. "This is no good," he said, almost to himself. "I need someone who can dance her behind off in front of that camera."

"Ow," Lila said again, trying to take another step. She was still determined to fill her role.

"You can't have my part," Lila yelled. She hobbled toward the director.

Andy Patman was looking from Lila to Jessica, then back again. "Wait, this just might work. It's worth a try." He turned to an assistant who was standing behind him. "Okay, these two are switching roles. Let's get them into wardrobe. I want to be rolling in ten."

"I did it," Jessica whispered to herself as she followed the assistant. "I am so *good!*"

Ten minutes later, Andy Patman was ready to film. Lila sat at the table on the kitchen set. Her crutches were nowhere in sight, and she had a big bowl of soup in front of her.

"All right, quiet, everyone! Places. And action!" Mr. Patman shouted his orders.

"I just love that show biz talk," Enid whispered to Elizabeth.

Everyone was silent as Lila began reciting her lines.

"Mmm," Lila said, sipping a spoonful of soup. "You know, being a teenager isn't easy. That's why I love to come home to a hot bowl of Holden tomato soup."

From offstage the music of the Holden soup jingle played. "When you're feeling hungry and your smile starts to droop, you know you need a shot of Holden tomato soup," a female voice sang.

As the music played, Jessica entered the kitchen set, dressed as a giant tomato. She looked completely ridiculous, and everyone on the sidelines burst into laughter.

Jessica continued to dance across the kitchen, a big smile on her face. But when she reached the far end of the kitchen, her huge costume bumped into the counter. The unexpected impact caused Jessica to career into a lighting stand, which fell, knocking into a dangling microphone.

As chaos erupted on the set Jessica slipped and fell. She bounced against the counter behind her, and a large basket of tomatoes fell from the shelf. The tomatoes tumbled onto Jessica's head and then rolled in every direction. Many of them splattered on the pristine kitchen floor, ruining the look of the set.

"Cut! Cut! Cut!" Andy Patman's outraged voice boomed through the cavernous studio.

As everyone collapsed with laughter Winston nudged Todd, who was sitting beside him. "Well, she did want the juicy part," Winston said.

The group fixed their eyes on Jessica, whose face was turning as red as her costume. She couldn't believe how much trouble she'd gone through to get a part as a dancing tomato in some stupid TV commercial!

Looking out at the laughing faces, Jessica vowed to herself that someday she *would* be a star. And when she got up to accept her first Academy Award for Best Actress, she'd conveniently forget to thank all of the "little people" who knew her before she made it big.

Jessica smiled to herself. Tomorrow was another day—and another chance to be in the spotlight!

SIGN UP FOR THE SWEET VALLEY HIGH® FAN CLUB!

Hey, girls! Get all the gossip on Sweet Valley High's® most popular teenagers when you join our fantastic Fan Club! As a member, you'll get all of this really cool stuff:

- Membership Card with your own personal Fan Club ID number
- A Sweet Valley High® Secret Treasure Box
- Sweet Valley High® Stationery
- Official Fan Club Pencil (for secret note writing!)
- Three Bookmarks
- A "Members Only" Door Hanger
- Two Skeins of J. & P. Coats® Embroidery Floss with flower barrette instruction leaflet
- Two editions of *The Oracle* newsletter
- Plus exclusive Sweet Valley High® product offers, special savings, contests, and much more!

Be the first to find out what Jessica & Elizabeth Wakefield are up to by joining the Sweet Valley High® Fan Club for the one-year membership fee of only $6.25 each for U.S. residents, $8.25 for Canadian residents (U.S. currency). Includes shipping & handling.

Send a check or money order (do not send cash) made payable to "Sweet Valley High® Fan Club" along with this form to:

SWEET VALLEY HIGH® FAN CLUB, BOX 3919-B, SCHAUMBURG, IL 60168-3919

NAME_____
(Please print clearly)

ADDRESS_____

CITY_____ STATE _____ ZIP_____
(Required)

AGE_____ BIRTHDAY_____ /_____ /_____

Offer good while supplies last. Allow 6-8 weeks after check clearance for delivery. Addresses without ZIP codes cannot be honored. Offer good in USA & Canada only. Void where prohibited by law.
©1993 by Francine Pascal   LCI-1383-123

Songs from
the Hit TV Series

Featuring:

"Rose Colored
Glasses"

"Lotion"

"Sweet Valley High
Theme"

SABAN
RECORDS

Available on CD and Cassette
Wherever Music is Sold.

Life after high school gets even *Sweeter!*

Francine Pascal's
SWEET VALLEY
SVU
UNIVERSITY
Life after high school gets even sweeter!

Jessica and Elizabeth are now freshmen at Sweet Valley University, where the motto is: Welcome to college — welcome to freedom!

Don't miss any of the books in this fabulous new series.

♥ College Girls #1	0-553-56308-4	$3.50/$4.50 Can.
♥ Love, Lies and Jessica Wakefield #2	0-553-56306-8	$3.50/$4.50 Can.
♥ What Your Parents Don't Know #3	0-553-56307-6	$3.50/$4.50 Can.
♥ Anything for Love #4	0-553-56311-4	$3.50/$4.50 Can.
♥ A Married Woman #5	0-553-56309-2	$3.50/$4.50 Can.
♥ The Love of Her Life #6	0-553-56310-6	$3.50/$4.50 Can.